THE GODDESS'S GAME

BOOK 1

THE GODDESS DIVINE SERIES

ALYSON ROSE

PROLOGUE

As Beth rounded the corner to her street, it took only a few steps and one deep breath for her to feel something was wrong. She stopped walking and looked behind her, not able to shake the feeling that she had been followed. She looked up the street and back over her shoulder one more time. Nothing. As she started in the direction of her house once more, she felt a warm breeze rush past her, and all at once the sidewalk in front of her disappeared.

Was that blue sky? she wondered.

It was! And it didn't take more than a second to know she was falling!

CHAPTER

ONE

Beth loved the winter. She loved the white of the snow, the frost in the air. But most of all she loved its unpredictability. You never knew what was going to happen on any given day when it came to the winter weather, especially in Montana.

Beth had lived in Montana most of her life. She'd moved from one end of the state to the other and lived in all kinds of places in the middle, but she'd yet to actually leave its borders. So this was a big step for her, going to Chicago.

She was happy to be going with her mother. She couldn't believe that when she'd asked to go with her mother on this real estate work trip, her mother had answered by saying, "I was actually going to ask you to come along. It will be a nice little vacation for us." She made it sound like it wasn't a huge deal. But she'd never let Beth come along before.

Her mother, Rena—although she was strict and seemed to know every thought that came into Beth's mind—was also Beth's best friend. It helped that her mother was extremely attractive and didn't look a day over twenty-five.

People often thought the two of them were sisters, and more than once it had gotten them a better table for dinner or moved them to the front of the line someplace. It was really kind of funny.

But as Beth got older, she couldn't help but notice she was the only one aging. She'd brought this up more than once to her mother, but Rena had just laughed it off, making some casual comment about how at least the teenaged Beth had that to look forward to. "Exceptional genes," she would say. Like with most things, Beth, just like her mother, laughed it off and was quietly thankful for "exceptional genes."

As Beth heard the plane's landing gear drop, she felt a flutter of butterflies in her stomach. This was it. Once this plane landed and she stepped outside, she would have finally been in two states in the United States of America. Really, it was three. But she decided she couldn't count the layover in North Dakota because she didn't actually set foot on the ground.

Beth heard the tires squeal and skid as they hit the pavement, and she felt the jolt of the plane as the pilots engaged the brakes. Slowly, the passing trees in the distance came to a stop.

"OK, let's go," Rena said once the plane had taxied to the gate. She stood, reached up, opened the overhead compartment, and grabbed both her small overnight bag and her daughter's. "Here you go, love."

"Thank you. I'm starving," Beth said.

"You're always starving," her mother replied with a large smile.

"Hey, I'm a growing girl."

"I don't think at eighteen you're still growing."

"Well, what can I say? Impeccable genes."

"Can't argue that, and you're very welcome," her mother said with a chuckle.

Beth was exactly one hundred and twenty pounds, five feet nine, with long black hair, not too curly but not too straight, with beautiful bronze skin that didn't require the sun in order to stay that wonderful color. Her mother was exactly the same height and weight, and they both had piercing green eyes. However, her mother's hair was naturally platinum blonde, almost to the point of being silver. And people noticed. Beth always wondered why she too didn't have that amazing feature, but she couldn't really complain. Her hair was as black as night and just like with her mother, people noticed.

Slowly, the line that had formed down the aisle started to move. One by one, the passengers started to exit while happy flight attendants thanked each and every person for flying with them this January morning.

As Beth and her mother made their way to the door, a gentleman still standing by his seat cut between them.

"Excuse me," he said before looking from Rena to Beth, clearly trying to decide if the two were sisters. "Twins?" he asked as they made their way down the aisle to the airplane's door.

"No," they both said in unison, making it apparent this was a question they got a lot.

"Just normal sisters?" the stranger continued.

"No," they said in unison again, making it clear they also got this a lot.

Finally, Beth answered while pointing, "Mother, daughter."

The gentleman looked a bit perplexed. "Really?" It was clear this was more curiosity than a question.

"Yes," Rena replied.

It was at that moment Beth realized she'd exited the plane and was standing in the hallway of the airport. Completely forgetting the man was there, she did a little dance while almost singing, "First time out of Montana! Gotta get a selfie!"

"Can it at least wait until we get our luggage?" her mother asked.

"Excuse me," the gentleman said before Beth could even answer her mother. "I don't mean to intrude. However, if this is your first time here, I would love to take the two of you out to eat. After all, there's no pizza like Chicago style."

Beth smiled at the gentleman. This was another thing she'd grown used to. She politely answered, "As much as I would love to take you up on that offer, my mother has taught me never to speak to strangers."

"Let alone eat with them," her mother chimed in with that almost sickly sweet voice she could get—the one that made it very clear she was a mother bear who needed you to move away from her cub. Now, please.

"OK, yeah. Sorry." The man stumbled over his words while quickly moving a safe distance away.

Beth just laughed. She turned to her mom. "You know, someday you're going to have to let me out of your sight, and that might require you trusting someone other than Dane."

Dane was Beth's godfather. Beth had always wondered why her mother and Dane hadn't gotten together. He was the only person her mother was truly herself around. He'd been a very present figure in their life as long as Beth could remember. Thanksgiving, Christmas, New Years, and birthdays, he was there. Anytime Beth brought it up, her mother just shushed her, almost in a tone that made Beth feel like she was being scolded. So she never pushed.

"Well, thank the goddess that day isn't today," her mother said.

Goddess. Another one of her mother's quirks. Rena never said "Thank God" or referred to any deity as a man; she always referred to a woman. And it always put a smile on Beth's face. She and her mother weren't religious people, but Beth always saw books about The Watchers—supposed fallen angels—lying around their house. And although her mother didn't read the Bible, she had several copies of *The Book of Enoch* in her bedroom. Beth had never actually talked to her mother about her choice of literature, but it was something she planned to ask about, not for any reason other than she was curious.

As they walked past all the shops that lined the corridor leading to baggage claim, Beth felt her excitement building again. She was actually going to see a city with skyscrapers, bridges, parks, and real Chinese food that could even be delivered. She was so ready for this.

Montana was beautiful and all, but it lacked the buzz— the buzz of all those people coming and going, the sound of car horns and sirens in the distance. Bits and pieces of busy people's conversations floating by as you passed them on the sidewalk. The streetlights flickering on and off as the daylight changed from dawn to dusk. Things were happening in the city, and Beth couldn't wait to be a part of it.

After grabbing their bags from the luggage area, they finally headed toward the glass doors that led outside. Beth was practically skipping.

Then she head a familiar voice behind her. "Slow down there, sunshine."

"Dane?" Beth said. She turned around, suddenly seeing

her godfather leaning up against the giant windows that lined the airport.

"I was in the neighborhood," he said.

"The neighborhood of Chicago," Beth's mom said in a rather dry tone, making it clear she meant it as a statement, not a question.

Beth looked around for where Dane could have possibly come from. There were no other terminals that led to this baggage area, and she knew for sure he hadn't been on their airplane. "Where did you come from?" she asked.

"Same place as you," he said, then started walking toward them, giving Beth and then her mother both a big hug.

"Which is where you were supposed to stay," Rena said, again making a statement in a tone that made it clear she wanted an explanation.

"Come on. How could you not want me here? It's me. Plus, I actually have business in town."

Beth's mother had a suspicious look on her face.

"Again, where did you come from?" Beth asked.

Both Dane and her mother started walking toward the open doors as if she'd said nothing at all. Beth followed in a hurried manner as soon as she realized the two of them were actually walking away. She was confused as to why they were ignoring her.

"Well, I hope you have your own hotel reservations. Beth and I are sharing a room, which means we don't have any extra space."

Dane chuckled and gave a quick salute toward Rena as he answered. "Absolutely, ma'am. Already taken care of."

"Does someone want to tell me what's going on?" Beth asked suddenly, almost startling her mother.

"Nothing, love. It looks like Dane has decided to join us on vacation."

"OK," Beth replied in her own suspicious tone. "Well, let's get this party started," she said while pretending to do the touchdown dance. Both Dane and her mother couldn't help but laugh.

"Yes, let's. I'm starving," Dane said. And with that, he clapped his hands and took a deep breath as if his nose would lead them to a restaurant.

CHAPTER

TWO

Beth had been so preoccupied by her godfather's arrival that she'd failed to notice she'd walked all the way to the rental car place without even looking up. Suddenly, she noticed all the activity going on around her.

"Let's rent a convertible so we can have the top down," she said as they stood at the counter, waiting to be helped.

"Honey, it's January in Chicago, and we're not having the top of our car missing," Rena replied.

"Why not? The cold doesn't bother us like it does other people," Beth said in a whiny tone. That was another thing that set Beth and Rena apart from other people—they both could tolerate very cold weather. Really, it wasn't even that they had a higher tolerance to low temperatures. They literally didn't feel a chill. Rena had always told her daughter it was, again, just fabulous genes. But she also always made it very clear that they shouldn't let people catch on. She would joke that they would end up being abducted by the CIA or NSA to be studied like lab rats.

"OK, fine," Beth said. "But how about a sunroof?"

"Deal," her mother said as a young gentleman came out of a back office. He walked toward the counter in a red rental-car shirt.

"Hello, how can I help you today?" he asked.

"We're needing a car for close to a month," Beth's mother replied while Beth poked her in the back, making it clear she wouldn't let her mother forget to ask about the sunroof.

"With a sunroof please, if you have one," Rena added.

"Of course we do. Do you have a reservation?"

"Actually, no. When I called, the gentleman I spoke to said there was no need."

"Normally that would be true. However, this week is the 2020 Millennium Art Festival. I'm sure your plane was packed. We have people who come from all over the United States for this."

Beth had noticed there wasn't a single seat open on the airplane. But really, why wouldn't people want to leave Montana? It hadn't seemed strange to her that the plane had been full.

"Well, is there anything you can do?" Rena continued. "We're really kind of depending on it."

"I would help you, but that means someone else will lose their reservation."

Dane stepped up to the counter, looking directly at the gentleman with that very intense stare of his. The young man immediately started typing while still looking at Dane.

"Are you sure there's nothing that can be done?" Dane asked in a quiet voice.

"Well, look at that. You're in luck. Looks like we do have an SUV we can get you," the man said, still not moving his eyes away from Dane's stare.

"With a sunroof?" Dane asked.

"Yes, of course, sir."

Beth looked from Dane to her mother with a clear question sitting on her face. Her mother just raised her hand as if to say, "Don't interrupt."

"Again, OK," Beth quietly said to herself. She'd seen some strange things happen around Dane and her mother, but nothing like this. This was like something out of a teenage vampire fantasy novel.

It looked like Dane had actually done some sort of voodoo mind meld with the guy. But when Beth looked back at the rental employee behind the counter, everything looked normal again. He was gathering a stack of papers from the printer and grabbing a set of keys from inside a glass cabinet.

"If you'll just sign here, initial here, and date this please," he said, while pointing at the papers. Beth's mother quickly scribbled her name and handed him her credit card.

She wouldn't ask now, but Beth made a mental note of the occasion. It wasn't likely she would forget, but she was going to ask about this.

Suddenly noticing that Dane was shaking a set of keys in her face, Beth pulled herself out of her head, instantly getting excited and giddy. Like a little kid, she grabbed the keys, again doing her touchdown dance as she started toward the doors that led to where the cars were all stored in a large garage. Rena and Dane followed close behind.

"This is going to be awsome!" Beth practically sang.

"Dane!" her mother shrieked. "She can't drive in the city!"

Both Beth and Dane stood still with no expression on their faces before looking at each other and bursting out laughing.

"Not giving these back!" Beth sang while shaking the keys in her mother's face. Just then she hit the alarm button on the key so they could look for one of the many SUVs sitting in front of them to light up. Startling all three of them, the black SUV directly in front of them beeped and flashed its lights.

Beth's jaw dropped. She couldn't believe this was the car. It was a beautiful, sleek black 2020 Cadillac Escalade with perfectly polished chrome all the way around it and tinted windows. She could just barely make out through the dark windows that there were TV screens in the leather seats.

She jumped toward the vehicle, opening the driver's-side door and exclaiming "OMG!" as she climbed in.

"Please use full sentences. We're not speaking valley girl emoji," her mother replied jokingly as she got in the front passenger seat.

"OH MY GODDESS!" Beth said, starting the vehicle. She shrieked again when she saw that the mileage meter read six miles. "We're the first people to drive this!" she sang out.

"Let's not be the first to wreck it," her mother said in that same joking tone while she clipped her seat belt and pretended to pull it tight as if she were on a roller coaster.

"Guess I'm in the back," Dane said. He laughed while getting in. He was clearly not nervous like Rena was about Beth driving through a major city for the first time.

Beth put the car in drive with a giant smile. "Ready?"

"No time like the present," Dane said, clearly encouraging Beth.

Suddenly the SUV jumped forward. Beth hit the brakes, stopping them just as suddenly.

"SLOWLY!" her mother shouted out.

"Sorry." Beth laughed, this time slowly easing out of the parking garage and heading for the street. "Which way am I going?" she asked.

Before her mother or Dane could answer, Beth saw the small screen to her right in the middle console light up and heard a woman's automated voice. "Please state location," the voice said.

Beth saw Dane perk up in her rearview mirror as he said, "2455 Blue Aster Lane, Lake Barrington, please."

Rena sat up straighter than she already was, if that was possible, and said, "I think we should save that for a little later in our trip."

"It's been eighteen years. She's ready."

With a look on her face that Beth thought almost looked like worry, her mother answered Dane by saying, "Then waiting a few more days wouldn't make much of a difference. Besides, Beth is hungry."

Staring at the path mapped out on the tiny screen, Beth again hit the gas and, deciding to follow the directions Dane had entered, turned left.

Rena gasped at the sudden change in direction.

"Sorry, Mom. We were holding up traffic. Anyways, what's the big deal? Whatever it is you two are discussing, it sounds like a surprise for me. And I looooooooove surprises even more than I love food."

"Alright," her mother said, looking a bit uneasy.

Dane, still wearing that little smirk he seemed to wear a lot around Beth's mother, just let out a little chuckle. "Like mother, like daughter," he said.

Rena, on the other hand was actually pleasantly surprised that Beth had managed to maneuver her way on and off the freeways. *It shouldn't have surprised me*, Rena thought. *Beth is good at everything she does.*

However, Beth didn't hear a word being said. She was much too busy taking in all the buildings and people surrounding them while they drove through the heart of Chicago. She'd never seen such a diversity of people. White, black, Asian, Indian—you name it, Beth saw it. She loved how differently everyone was dressed. She herself was just a T-shirt-and-jeans girl, as was pretty much every other girl in Montana, but she hoped that one day, and one day soon, she would adopt some of the fashion she was seeing around her in Chicago.

"So where are we going?" Beth asked her mother as she continued to follow the automated female voice.

"You said you liked surprises."

"Mom! Come on."

"What?" Rena replied as she looked out the windows.

"Come on. Someone tell me where we're going. Joking aside, I really would like to know, and this trip has already been off to a strange start."

"Hey, I'm not a strange start to your trip," Dane said with a laugh.

Beth said, in a loud and sudden tone, "That's not what I meant!" at the exact same time her mother said, in the exact same tone, "That's not what she meant!"

Throwing his hands in the air like he was giving up, Dane laughed, enjoying the ruffled feathers.

THREE

Michael walked down the gravel road, following it as it wound down and around the old, abandoned wooden buildings that had probably been there for well over a hundred years. He'd always wondered how they were still standing. The wind out in these parts of Montana sometimes reached what felt like hurricane strength, and although the buildings were definitely leaning toward the ground, they never actually fell over. Even with the snow piled so thick on the failing roofs, they stood.

Michael stopped, taking in the warm sun on his face. Closing his eyes, he reached out with his mind and listened to the silence. Very slowly, he started to hear the crunch of snow beneath a large buck that was standing so close to him that he felt like he could walk directly up to it and touch it. Its rack was large, making it clear it had survived many winters already. Michael heard the sound of a large snow owl taking flight, no doubt looking for a place to hole up and sleep for the day before hunting at night.

Michael smiled. He spent all year waiting to be able to

finally come out here and spend time with his dad. He never liked leaving his mother for long. She depended on him, but he figured she could manage him being gone one month out of the year—especially now that he was done with school and had been done for two years now. Normally he would have come during the summer months while school was out. However, now that he had graduated, he'd decided to come early, during the winter months, and enjoy the untouched snow of the prairies. After this trip, he would have to consider whether he was going to go on to community college or leave his mother permanently and move out here to help his father full-time with the ranch. He'd been quite surprised when his father had asked him to move out, and it was something Michael was really considering. Yes, he loved the city of Billings most days, but nothing was as comforting as being out on the prairies of Montana. They might look like nothing at all was going on, but if you really stopped and listened, there was so much life out there. Although he didn't have the best relationship with his father, Michael wouldn't give up the time he got to spend out there for anything. He knew he looked out of place in this small town—if you could really call it a town. A post office, a small store, and a local bar was all there was —and a ton of purebred cowboys. He had to start his life at some point. And he'd be only six hours away. He figured his mother could manage, and he'd still be close enough to visit and look in on her often.

Michael had been blessed with a birthmark directly on the top of his head, making it so that his jet-black hair had a perfect white strip growing through it. He figured it must have been genetic, because his father had the same birthmark. Although, his father's was much larger, or at least seemed to have gotten much larger the older he'd gotten.

Michael had tried many times when he was younger to dye it all kinds of colors, but the white hair just wouldn't hold the dye longer than a single wash.

As he got older, he'd learned to love the uniqueness of it. But in a town like this, full of cowboys, it drew a lot of unwanted attention from the younger and the older crowds—especially when Michael decided to have a night out at the local bar, now finally being twenty-one and old enough to partake. Nevertheless, overall, he didn't mind. He couldn't explain it. He always felt that maybe, just maybe, the white strip meant more than he could know yet.

He continued to follow the gravel road until it disappeared and turned into a ranch trail. The wind howled, making tall snowdrifts that looked like frozen waves crashing on a white beach.

Just then, he heard someone calling. "Michael! Michael, where are you?"

"Here, just on my way up now!" Michael closed his eyes and took in the warm sunshine on his face for one last second—one more second that belonged just to him. Then he ran up the ranch trail to where his father was waiting in Old Blue, the beat-up ranch truck. Michel laughed. His father could definitely afford any truck he liked, but he chose to drive a 1968 GMC flatbed. He probably spent more time working on it in a year than he did driving it.

Michael ran alongside the truck, which was still slightly moving, and jumped in.

"We're in a hurry, son. Don't want to miss the plane," his dad said.

"Plane? I just got here. Where are we going?"

"Chicago."

"Chicago? You've got to be kidding me. Really? I get one month. One month, Dad."

His father raised an eyebrow and, with a rather gruff voice, said, "Dad?"

"Excuse me. I meant sir. Sir, I only have one month up here. What could possibly be so important in Chicago that we would need to go there? Have you ever even been to Chicago, sir?"

"Son, why do you come to my ranch every year?"

"What do you mean? You're my father. That should be self-explanatory."

"Let's say it's not. Why do you come up here every winter?"

"I have a feeling you already have a rebuttal for whatever I might say. So let's just jump to that part."

His father just sighed, too rundown from his daily routine on the ranch to keep up the banter. "You come to learn—learn the ways of the land, air, and water. To speak its languages so you'll be prepared for whatever comes your way once I'm gone and you're in the position to carry on our name. You're also here to be the teacher when I'm no longer."

"OK. Wow. That was way deeper than I was expecting. If whatever's in Chicago is what spurred that little speech, then by all means, we better go."

"Smart-ass," his father replied with a smile and a loving look in his eye.

"You know it, sir, you know it," Michael replied. "So now that we've had this father-son heart-to-heart, can you please tell me why we're going to Chicago"?

"There's a girl. Beth, I believe her name is," his father said. "And she'll be having her coming-of-age ceremony."

"OK. But that happens all the time, and I don't think we've ever even been to one."

"You're right, but this is the daughter of Rena McCarther."

Michael sat straight up and was silent. He felt like he should ask again if his father had actually said Rena McCarther, but he knew he'd definitely heard his father clearly. Instead, the only question he came up with was, "What's the daughter's name?"

"I already told you that. It's Beth," his father replied.

"Beth?" Michael smirked. "She's the descendant of a sacred goddess, and her name is Beth"? "Supposed descendant, remember. And I can't say I disagree about the name being odd. But, in defense of her mother, she wanted to raise the girl as an ordinary person. And Beth seems like a very ordinary name."

"Wait, are you saying this girl has no idea who or what she is? Because I can't really think of anything worse than keeping that kind of information regarding your child's destiny hidden from them for eighteen years."

"Doesn't matter what we think. It's what Rena wanted for her. But either way, she'll find herself and her true name when she eats the apple at her ceremony at the end of this month."

"End of the month, and we're leaving today? So I guess this isn't going to be a quick trip. Great, just great."

FOUR

Beth, truly enjoying the drive, looked over at her mother, noticing she didn't seem to be enjoying herself at all. She was looking out the window but didn't seem to be actually seeing what was there. She seemed to be a million miles away, someplace in her mind.

"Mom?"

No answer

"Mom?" Beth said with a little more force.

From the back seat, Dane gently put his hand on her mother's shoulder and quietly whispered, "Rena?"

That seemed to snap her out of it. "Yes" she said, looking over at Beth while holding on to Dane's hand.

"You OK, Mom?" Beth asked.

"Of course. Forgive me. I was far away, remembering things from a long time ago."

"Care to share?" Beth softly asked.

Dane, chiming in from the back seat, answered the question. "I think the jet lag may be catching up to your mother, love. Why don't we let her close her eyes for a few minutes while we drive."

"Jet lag? The flight was like two hours." Beth laughed while looking in the rearview mirror at Dane and realizing he was definitely not laughing.

"OK, weird," Beth mouthed. One minute her mom was her normal, bubbly self, and now she was acting like a fragile bird learning to fly. This confused Beth because her mother was the strongest woman she knew.

"I think I'll close my eyes for just a moment or two," Rena said. "I think you're right about the jet lag. We have about forty-five minutes left in our drive anyway." With that being said, Rena leaned on the door and closed her eyes, seeming to fall asleep quickly.

Dane sat back, crossing his hands behind his head, and closed his eyes, looking very comfortable all of the sudden. "Wake me up if you get lost, little lady," he said. Then he dropped his sunglasses over his eyes, making it clear he would probably be snoring like a kid in a car seat very soon.

Beth continued to drive and turned on the radio quietly, so as not to disturb the two sleeping beauties. As she looked out the window, she started to take note of all the things she would never see in Montana. For example, walking down the sidewalk was a woman pushing a full-size grocery shopping cart filled all the way to the brim with aluminum cans and other sorts of trash. She looked as though she probably hadn't seen the inside of a shower in weeks. Maybe months.

Beth cringed when she thought about how bad the poor homeless women must smell. Then she immediately scolded herself for having such a judgmental thought. But there was one thing Beth had noticed about the woman: even though her clothes were tattered, dirty, and old and she was surrounded by seagulls trying to get at the trash in the shopping cart, she had the largest and most genuine smile. It looked as though in her mind she was carrying a Gucci handbag, wearing a fur coat, and having a fantastic day of shopping. Beth realized that smile made her the most beautiful woman on the block.

"Funny, isn't it?"

Beth jumped, hearing Dane's voice all of the sudden from the back seat. She looked in her rearview mirror and saw that he still had his glasses on and was leaning back like he was asleep.

"Isn't what funny?" she replied.

"Exactly what you were thinking about the woman on the street—how she seems to be totally content and yet surrounded by what most people would consider junk."

"But I didn't say that out loud."

"It really shows you just how relative it all actually is." Dane continued talking as though Beth had said nothing at all. "One person's delight could be another's misery, and vice versa."

Although he made a very valid and deep point regarding the human condition, Beth was still focused on the fact that she hadn't spoken out loud. It seemed to her that Dane had read her mind. Sure, he did some strange stuff from time to time, but this by far surpassed them all. Then Beth remembered the encounter with the car rental guy. *OK*, she thought, *maybe this is the second strangest thing.* Glancing back in her mirror once more, she saw he was now smiling, still with the dark sunglasses on, but definitely smiling as if he'd just heard her contemplating all of this in her head. Then he laughed out loud.

In response, like the teenager she was, Beth just turned the radio louder and drove a little faster.

After what seemed like forever, they finally managed to make their way through traffic and get to the outskirts of the city. The houses were starting to look larger and larger the farther they went. Beth looked over at her sleeping mother and, almost as if on cue, Rena opened her eyes, let out a little yawn, and stretched. Then she looked around as if to orient herself.

"We're close," she said. She seemed to be back to her normal self, but Beth could still hear an undertone of worry or nervousness in her voice.

"Where's here?" Beth asked. "I can tell you're stressed for some reason, but this is supposed to be a vacation, and nothing on a vacation should be making you nervous, Mom."

Rena looked as though she was just about to open her mouth to speak when the car's GPS voice said, "In one quarter mile, your destination will be on the right."

Beth looked down the road, and her mouth dropped open. This house they were heading to wasn't just the biggest house on the block. This was the biggest house Beth had ever seen.

In a very matter-of-fact voice, Beth's mother all of the sudden said, "Beth, you're correct. I am nervous. And I'm nervous because you're about to meet your father."

If Beth's mouth hadn't already been open due to the enormity of the home whose driveway she was turning into, it would have again hit the ground and probably shattered like ice.

As she set the parking brake in the driveway, Beth managed to spit out, "My father? I think this just went from fun family vacation to WHAT COULD YOU POSSIBLY BE TALKING ABOUT?"

But before her mother could do or say anything, Beth was again surprised by a knock on her window. In absolute shock, she rolled it down to find herself staring at a tan-skinned man impeccably dressed in a pinstripe suit, something Beth imagined a young Lucky Luciano would have worn. He was staring directly at her with eyes as green as emeralds—eyes she recognized because she saw them every day when she looked in the mirror. This man was young—young in the same way her mother was young—and he, too, had platinum-blond hair that almost glowed silver like her mother's. However, unlike her mother, he had a single strip of raven-black hair that grew directly in front, making his eyes look that much more piercing.

Beth turned to her mother with a stunned look. In somewhat of an ornery tone, she said, "I guess we know where my black hair comes from now."

FIVE

Michael jumped out of the truck, quickly ran into the ranch house, and grabbed a bag from the closet in his room to pack—a bag he'd just unpacked a few days before. From the closet he also pulled out his one and only nice suit and gently placed it in the bag. Then, in no organized fashion at all, he threw his everyday clothes from the dresser on top of the suit and zipped the bag closed. After grabbing a few last things from the bathroom, he ran back down the stairs and out to the truck.

"Did you remember to grab your salve? You don't want your mark of origin to fade," Michael's father said.

"It's been six months. It's unlikely it would fade now. But yes, I did, sir," Michael answered as he pulled up his right sleeve and gazed at the glistening ink of what looked like a brand-new tattoo that covered his forearm. It was of a giant gray wolf with a map of the constellation Canis Major within its borders. Michael was still in awe of the artwork and what it meant. The few of his kind who'd survived the Great Catastrophe of his planet and managed to make it to

Earth could all shift, but now they said the blood of their kind had become so diluted with the blood of humans that not all inherited the ability. Michael had always known deep down that he would be able to shift, but when he finally came of age and the change happened, he'd been secretly relieved.

It was only after the first change that the tattoo was received. The ink came from the dust of a meteorite that had hit the Earth the same day their people landed after years of aimlessly wandering the stars, trying to find a new home where they could survive. Finally, the Earth had come into view behind the giant floating rock, almost as if it was rising out of the blackness like a lighthouse. Michael had heard the story so many times that he felt like he himself had lived it.

No one knew what form they would take when the change happened. Some took on the form of a wolf, others a bear, and some even the form of an eagle. The tattoos were a way to recognize one another. Those who didn't shift were still tattooed with the sacred ink, but instead of an animal, they wore three stars in the shape of a triangle with a circle in the middle to symbolize the home they'd been forced to flee. A special salve made by the medicine man of the Hopi people kept the body from rejecting the ink and the tattoo from fading.

"Either way, it's best to bring it," his father replied. "We have one last stop to make before we leave. It looks like part of the herd has found a way past the eastern fence. We need to round them up quickly."

Michael smiled. Any chance he got to shift was a chance he didn't pass up.

SIX

Beth slowly opened her door as her mother reached over and popped the hatch before exiting the vehicle herself. Dane jumped out of the back seat and put his hand out to the gentleman standing next to the car.

"Good to see you, Brad. Long time no see," he said.

"You look good. Guardianship has agreed with you," the man answered.

"Well, you know. Someone's got to do it."

The gentleman chuckled slightly but didn't actually look amused. He quickly turned his attention to Rena, who looked like a deer caught in headlights.

"You look amazing, Rena. Not that I would expect anything else."

"Thank you, Brad. It's been a good eighteen years."

Beth looked at Brad's intense stare into her mother's eyes. She couldn't tell if he was being genuine or passive-aggressive. If he really was her father, Beth guessed he was being passive-aggressive. It was a trait that seemed to run thick in her mother and, if she was being honest, herself as well.

"Um, I don't mean to break up the happy reunion, but will one of you please tell me what's going on?" Beth interjected.

Brad immediately turned his attention to Beth. She almost took a step back once that intense stare was on her.

"My name is Brad McCarther. I'm your father. I'm sure this is all very confusing to you, but let me say that you're exactly as I pictured you would be."

"Yeah, fantastic," Beth said under her breath, realizing everyone was staring at her. She quickly turned to her mother. "So, I'm going to start with, Why am I just now hearing about this?"

"Let's go inside and get settled, and we can all sit down and discuss everything, OK?" Rena said.

"Get settled? We're staying here? What about the hotel?" Beth asked.

"Yes, I think that would be best," Brad interrupted.

Beth wasn't sure how to respond. This had transitioned from a family vacation and long-awaited trip to The Cheesecake Factory into a life-altering therapy session within just a few minutes.

Beth suddenly felt Dane standing behind her as he quietly said, "Trust me. This will all make sense soon, and you'll be happy you're here. This is the safest place you could be."

"Safest? I didn't realize I was ever not safe," Beth said. Her tone now started to match her confusion as her irritation grew.

Rena grabbed her daughter's hand. "Let's just try it," she said. "I'll keep the reservation at the hotel just in case, OK?"

"Fine, but I want to order Chinese food," Beth responded in a somewhat defiant voice even though she knew it sounded childish. Then she started walking to the front door, pausing and looking back when she realized no one was following her.

"Are you coming?" she asked.

At that, everyone started toward the front door. As Beth reached out to grab the doorknob, the door suddenly opened, and she saw a short bald man in a suit standing off to the side.

"Welcome home, miss," he said quietly. "Where are your bags? I'm happy to show you to your rooms."

"Rooms? I get more than one?"

The man smiled and answered, "Yes, the north apartment has been made up for you and your mother. There are two bedrooms, a kitchen, and a wonderful living area."

Beth slowly took in the grand scene before her and realized this house was large enough to probably have a few apartments in it. The floor was a wonderful granite-looking type of tile, polished so perfectly that Beth could clearly see her reflection in it. There was a giant double staircase in the foyer. What looked like a family portrait hung on the wall between the two sets of stairs. Beth quickly recognized her mother and Brad in the photo. Hearing the others enter the house behind her, she pointed to the portrait as if to ask a question while looking at her mother.

"Let's get to our rooms," her mother said in response to the look on Beth's face.

"I'll send Marco up to get you when lunch is ready," Brad said. "Take some time to get comfortable." He smiled at Beth, then quickly walked off in the direction of a room that was to the right of the foyer.

"Marco? Who's Marco?" she asked.

"That would be me, miss," said someone from behind a stack of their luggage. There the short bald man stood, trying to carry the many bags brought in from the SUV. With what seemed like a giant effort, he hoisted all of the bags up and said, "Right this way, miss."

"Beth. You can call me Beth."

The man smiled and continued toward the stairs, choosing the set that led to the left. "Wonderful," he replied. "Right this way, Beth."

When they reached the top of the staircase, they followed Marco down a long hallway that had several closed doors on the left and giant windows on the right that overlooked an enormous indoor garden with a pool directly in the middle of it.

"There's a pool," Beth said, not really to anybody, but Marco answered anyway.

"Yes, that's for your private use. Your father has his own on the other side of the grounds."

"Fancy," Dane said in a somewhat smart-ass tone.

Marco pretended not to hear Dane's comment and opened the door directly at the end of the hallway, setting the bags off to the right and waiting for everyone to enter the apartment.

Beth was in awe of how large it actually was. The ceiling was high, just like the ceilings in the foyer. The kitchen was directly off to the right and looked like your typical kitchen, with beautiful countertops and expensive appliances. The living room, which was right in front of them, had a thick white carpet, a large couch, and two recliners. A big-screen TV hung on the wall. Marco pointed to two remote controls that sat on the small coffee table in front of the couch.

"This one will turn on the TV, and this one will turn on

the entertainment system. Over in this cubby here," he said, opening a large sliding door that looked more like a closet than a cupboard, "you'll find all the newest movies. If there's something you would like to watch that you don't see, just let me know."

"I'm sure that will be just fine," Rena said.

"Is that an actual smart fridge?" Beth asked.

"Yes, miss. Top of the line."

"Wow, cool!"

"If you follow me, I'll show you two your bedrooms."

They followed Marco down the short hallway, which had two rooms directly at the end.

"This would be your room, Beth. The bathroom connects the two bedrooms directly through that door," Marco said, pointing.

Beth's room had a queen-size bed with light-blue bedding and a small nightstand. There was a large closet off to the left and a large TV on the wall.

"The controls for this TV are just there on the night-stand," Marco said.

With that, he set Beth's three large bags on the bed and proceeded to the other bedroom to set down her mother's bags. Before he left, he turned in the direction of Beth's mother and said, "Rena, it's nice to see you after all these years. I can tell you've done a good job with the young one,."

He tipped his head as if to excuse himself and turned to leave. But he stopped just before closing the door. "I'll be back in an hour, once lunch is ready. If you need anything, please press this button. You can also use it, Dane, when you're ready to be taken to your rooms." He pointed to what looked like a tiny computer screen next to the door that was lit up with call buttons labeled for different rooms in the house.

"Thank you, Marco," Rena replied with a smile. And with that, Marco closed the door and left. Dane had already made himself comfortable on the couch and was messing with the remotes, trying to get the TV on. Suddenly the room was filled with extra-loud white noise.

"Dane!" Beth squealed while covering her ears.

He quickly hit the volume button, muting the sound. "Whoops, sorry about that."

"Can we please turn that off? If you hadn't guessed, I have a million questions. And to be honest, I'm getting overwhelmed. And that's leading to me getting pissed off."

"No problem. You call the shots, kiddo," Dane replied, clicking the TV back off.

"Thank you," Beth said in a somewhat exasperated tone. "Now, Mom. Start talking," Beth said, staring directly at her mother with a look on her face that made it clear she wanted answers now.

Rena walked over and sat next to Dane on the couch, gesturing for Beth to sit down as well. Beth sat in one of the recliners, making a mental note of how comfortable it was and that it was probably the perfect place for a nap.

"OK," Rena said. "I guess there's no easy way to start this, so I'll just start. That man, Brad McCarther, is your father. As you've probably guessed, this side of the family is pretty well off."

Beth didn't respond, making it clear she just wanted to hear the truth.

"Beth, this is going to sound pretty crazy, so just bear with me, OK?" Rena paused briefly. Then, gesturing to the three of them, she said, "We're not from this planet originally. Yes, you were born here, but our kind aren't native to this world. We look like humans, with the exception of our hair color and our bright eyes. And we have abilities humans don't have."

"Abilities?" Beth asked, her tone now bordering on disbelief. She almost laughed out loud at the absurdity of it all.

"Yes, like reading each other's thoughts," Rena replied.

Beth suddenly jumped up out of her chair like she'd been shocked. She felt her heart pounding in her chest. She'd just heard her mother speak, she was sure of it. But her mother's lips hadn't moved.

"It's OK, honey. After your coming-of-age ceremony, you'll be able to communicate this way as well."

"Coming-of-age ceremony?" Beth repeated. "Why does it feel like everything you say is coming out of a fantasy novel?" Beth slowly sat down, realizing that her mother was speaking to her, but her lips had yet to move.

"OK, let's back up just a bit," Dane interjected. "Let's start with who we are."

"OK, who are we?" Beth asked.

"We're the Annu, a humanoid species from a planet that orbited the star Sirius B. Tarrin is what our people called it. Twelve thousand years ago, we were forced to leave due to the Great Catastrophe."

"Which was?" Beth asked.

"One of our three moons, Eba, was struck by a large asteroid and broke up into many, many pieces. Not only did Eba control the tides on our planet, but now it was broken into pieces that had unstable orbits. They could have hit Tarrin and ripped it apart. We didn't have much time to come up with a plan to try and save our people. So as many of us that could fit boarded the few ships we had and set out to find a new home. For many years, the Annu wandered the stars, hoping and praying to the goddess that they could find a home. Finding Earth was like being rescued from a death sentence. When the Annu first landed here, they weren't aware that the planet already had a humanoid species living on it. But they were nothing like they are today. They lived in small groups and had no concepts of farming or building. It was agreed by the elders that we would help move the species along the best we could without introducing any kind of violence or anything that could be used for malevolent purposes. It was also agreed that they wouldn't know all of our capabilities—especially that the Annu can shift."

"Shift?" Beth whispered, almost afraid to ask.

"Yes. Shift, honey," her mom said. And with that, a warm breeze swept through the room. Beth saw a bright glow start to emanate from her mother just before a whirlwind seemed to envelop her. Suddenly, Beth wasn't looking at her mother. She was looking at a giant golden eagle, only it was many times larger and had her mother's eyes. Beth jumped to her feet, almost involuntarily, and felt herself get light-headed and her knees give out. Yep, she was having an anxiety attack and passing out. Her mom had just turned into a bird.

"Oh my goddess," was all Beth could say before everything went black and she hit the floor with a thud.

SEVEN

As the truck pulled up along the side of the fence, it was clear how the cattle had gotten out. There was a large section of the fence that was rolled back from where one of the barbed-wire strands had broken.

"This almost looks cut," Michael said while investigating the breakage.

"Nah, I think it just rusted through," his father replied.

"I don't see the cattle. How far do you think they made it?"

"Can't be too far, but the longer we stand here, the farther they'll get. Why don't you go round 'em up, and I'll repair this fence. Run them through the north gate and head back here."

"Sure thing," Michael replied.

A warm breeze rushed passed Michael's father as a bright light started to glow around Michael. Then, within the blink of an eye, it was no longer Michael standing by the fence. It was giant gray wolf, easily three times the size of any wolf in the wild, with a beautiful white star in its fur directly between his eyes. In his mind, Michael heard his father say, "No hunting. We don't have time. Just round 'em up."

And with that, the giant wolf bounded off with his nose to the ground, tracking the missing cattle.

This was Michael's favorite state of being. He loved how he could hear anything and everything, and how he could smell specific scents, not just the jumbled mess his human nose could smell. But most of all, he loved to run. He loved to feel the vibration of the earth when his paws lightly touched the ground and how that vibration changed when another animal was close.

Michael continued to follow the scent of the cattle, careful to stay upwind. His father was right—they weren't far, but he couldn't see them yet. As he crested a large hill, they suddenly came into view. They were all huddled in a group around a man-made water hole. Slowly, so as not to startle them, Michael came up on the group. He could sense their uneasiness as he came closer, so he gently rubbed his nose along the largest female's side, sensing her strong heartbeat and trying to give her some reassurance that he wasn't there to hurt them. One by one, he went from cow to cow, lightly rubbing his nose alongside them while softly nudging them in the direction of the ranch. It took a little coaxing, but they slowly started to walk. Michael could sense their understanding as the cattle started to move more quickly. Following them, Michael made sure to keep an eye on the two small calves that were barely a few months old. He chuckled in his mind as they tried to keep up, unsure of their footing.

Off in the distance, Michael suddenly heard the loud shriek of a bird. But it wasn't just any bird. It was an eagle —one of their eagles. He ran quickly to the front of the herd while looking up in the sky, so high, he could barely see the giant bald eagle. He could see it was circling something off in the distance. Sensing that something was very off, Michael reached out with his mind, trying to hear his father. No other shifters Michael knew of should be this far north.

Hearing nothing in his mind from his father, Michael started to rush the herd, pushing them into a full-on run. Trying to keep the eagle in his sight, Michael realized as the bird circled that it was darting to the ground and rising in the sky again and again. He quickly returned to his human form and rushed to unlock the gate, hurrying the cattle as quickly as he could and locking the gate behind them.

Then, as fast as he could, Michael took off at a dead run, shifting once again. Again, he reached out with his mind to his father and realized he was hearing his father faintly call for help. Michael's heart pounded in his chest so loud that the rushing blood in his ears was drowning out the sound of his father's voice. He watched as the giant bird dove and reappeared over and over. Michael could now see its beak was covered in a glistening bright-red substance, and the thick smell of iron was in the air.

Blood, lots of blood.

Michael ran as fast as his legs would allow him—so fast his paws barely touched the ground. The closer he got, the louder his father's voice became. Michael could now see his father had shifted into his wolf form but was clearly injured. His hind legs had both gone limp, but he was still forcefully snapping his powerful jaws as the eagle continued to pierce his skin with its sharp beak. His father's strength was waning. Michael watched as the giant bird took one final dive, boring its beak deep in his father's chest. His father let out a painful yelp as his whole body dropped to the dirt.

Michael dove, baring his teeth and snapping his jaw, just a split second too slow to catch the giant eagle as it took off into the sky, flapping its powerful wings.

Michael immediately shifted back into his human form and rushed to his father's side.

"Sir, can you hear me?" he asked while putting pressure on the gaping wound bleeding in the giant wolf's chest. His father was limp, with his tongue hanging to the side. Michael shook him again. "Father, Father, please answer me."

Very faintly in his mind, he heard his father speak.

"Be there when she eats the apple. You must keep her safe."

With that, his father let out a final whimper, and his eyes turned to glass.

He'd passed.

Michael sat quietly, trying to understand what had happened. Murder was not only strictly forbidden by his kind, but it was the worst offence that could be committed. To end the life of a soul before the goddess called them home was to say you, the murderer, were godlike yourself —that you should decide when a soul's journey should end.

Michael picked up his father's limp body, his heart aching with every step, and gently set him in the back of the flatbed. Then he proceeded to drive back to the ranch house. He would bury his father and go to Chicago like he'd been asked. Then, however long it took and wherever it took him, he wouldn't stop until he found justice for his father.

EIGHT

Beth's vision was still blurry, and she had a giant lump on her head from hitting the floor so hard and fast. Just inches from her nose was her mother's panicked face. Rena's lips weren't moving, but Beth could clearly hear her in her mind.

"Oh, I knew this was going to be too much. Honey, can you hear me? Squeeze my hand if you can hear me."

"Mom, I can hear you, but can you please use your mouth to speak for a minute? I need some normality while I regain my senses."

"OK. Sorry, honey. Here, let me help you up. Or do you need to stay lying down?"

"No. Mom, stop fussing," Beth answered while batting her mother's hand away from her face.

"Rena, why don't we just give her a minute? Maybe we should answer her questions before we go any further," Dane kindly interrupted.

Just as Beth was about to speak, there was a knock at the door. Dane jumped up from where the three of them were huddled on the floor and opened the door.

"Lunch is served," Marco politely stated as he looked past Dane at Rena and Beth.

"Great. I'm starving," Dane said while rubbing his belly.

"Can we have a minute?" Rena asked.

"Of course," Marco replied while closing the door. The look of concern on his face made it apparent he would be waiting on the other side.

"Honey, are you sure you feel up for lunch?" Rena asked Beth..

"Yes. Food is the only thing I feel very sure about right now," she replied just as her stomach let out an extra-large growl.

"OK. We can finish our talk once you get some food in you," her mother said.

"I can't wait," Beth said while laughing in a way that made it clear she was nervous. She went into the bathroom, quickly changed her clothes, and threw her hair up in a tight ponytail. While looking in the mirror, she took a moment just to breathe. She wondered if she too could shift into a bird. *Or would it be something else? Could they shift into more than one animal?* she wondered. That was something she would have to remember to ask.

Beth laughed in disbelief. *Who would have thought I would be having a serious conversation about shifting into an animal and living on other planets? Not to mention that I'd be on my way to eat lunch with a man who, up until three hours ago, didn't exist.*

Beth wondered why she wasn't more freaked out. She imagined other people in this situation would be in an all-out panic right about now, or angry. But she felt oddly comfortable already with the idea that Brad McCarther was her father. It felt like a missing piece of the puzzle had fallen into place.

"Honey, are you ready?" Beth suddenly heard her mother in her head. Even though she wasn't in the room, she clearly heard her speak in her mind.

"Mom!" she called through the closed door. "Too soon! Please talk to me like we're normal people."

"Honey, as you'll learn at lunch, most of the Annu rarely speak out loud."

Beth quickly opened the bathroom door she'd been hiding behind to find her mother standing in the doorway with a stance that made it clear she was waiting impatiently.

"Wait. Does this mean you can read my thoughts? Like, you know everything I'm thinking?" Beth asked in a somewhat panicked tone.

"No. It doesn't work like that. We only hear what you wish. But until your ceremony, the connection only goes one way," Beth heard Dane answer in her mind.

"Oh thank the goddess," Beth replied in a joking tone.

"I hate to interrupt, but are we ready for lunch?" Marco asked as he poked his head in the apartment door.

At that moment, Beth's stomach let out another giant growl as if to answer the question itself.

"I think that means yes," Dane answered, and the three of them shuffled out of the apartment behind Marco.

"I hope you like fish. We're serving a wonderful baked Alaskan halibut today," Marco said.

"Fish?" Beth asked. "In Chicago? That seems—"

"That sounds wonderful. We love halibut," Rena said, apologizing for Beth's bluntness with her chipper tone.

Beth again heard her mother in her mind. "I know this is a lot, but it's no reason to be rude."

Fantastic, Beth thought. *Now she can scold me not only out loud but in my mind as well.*

"Fish sounds great," Beth said with a smile, immediately seeing Marco light up, happy he'd pleased them.

They continued back down the stairs, through the foyer, and out a set of large glass doors that led to an enormous indoor atrium that sat directly below the window of the apartment they were staying in. Beth was in awe of the magnificent flowers and perfectly groomed gardens.

"This place is amazing," she said.

"Glad you approve," she heard Brad reply.

"Hello, Brad," her mother said while elbowing Beth.

"Hello, sir," Beth said, giving Brad a quick smile.

"I hope you're hungry. Marco has a wonderful lunch planned."

"We heard. Fish," Beth replied in a somewhat monotone voice.

Brad just smiled while gesturing toward a table that was set up on the patio. Beth immediately tried to stifle a laugh when she saw the place setting—each person had three forks and several spoons. *How much are we eating?* she wondered. She also saw little placement cards with their names neatly written on them, assigning each person a place to sit.

"Ma'am," Marco said while pulling out a chair for Beth.

"Thank you," Beth replied while sitting.

Marco then pulled out a second chair on the other side of the table. "For you, Rena."

"Thank you. You're too sweet."

Pulling out his own chair, Dane jokingly said, "Don't worry about me. I got it."

It was clear this type of humor was lost on Marco. He simply looked at Dane and walked in the other direction, which Beth assumed was toward the kitchen.

After seating himself at the head of the table, Brad

turned his attention to Beth. "How did you like the apartment?"

"Cozy," Beth answered.

"Well, if there's anything you need or want, all you need to do is ask."

"I'd like to know where you've been the last eighteen years," Beth replied in a less-than-enthusiastic tone.

"Beth!" her mother snapped.

"No, it's alright," Brad said. "Straight to business. I like it. I don't much care for small talk myself."

"I guess we have that in common," Beth said.

"I think you'll find we have a lot in common," Brad replied.

Marco returned with three plates in each hand—plates containing something that smelled absolutely wonderful. Placing two plates of appetizers in the middle of the table and a salad in front of each person, Marco asked what he could get each person to drink.

"We have Coke products, Pepsi products, mineral water, and, of course, something stronger for the adults if you would like," he said.

"It's lunchtime," Rena answered in a somewhat shocked tone.

"You're right. Not before noon," Brad said with a laugh.

"I'll take a Jack and Coke minus the Jack," Beth said.

"Cute," her mother replied.

"Don't I know it?" Beth said with a small smirk.

"I'll take a Coke as well," Dane cut in.

"Mineral water, please," Rena finally said.

And with that, Marco hurried out of the atrium again. Beth started to eat her salad while keeping an eye on Brad, the look on her face making it clear she was waiting for him to start talking.

"Where have I been? Was that the question?" he said.

Beth didn't answer. She just waited.

"Well." He hesitated, as if to find the right words. "My job, we'll call it, takes me many places and at times could have put you in great danger. Your mother and I agreed it would be best to spare you chaos as long as possible. To give you as normal an upbringing as we could. Your future has many challenges ahead. So we wanted you to have a peaceful childhood and nurture your gifts without fear."

"Gifts. You mean the mind reading I can't do yet?"

"No. I mean your connection to nature and the goddess."

"How was that nurtured when you guys have told me nothing about any of this my whole life?"

"When you're out in nature, how do you feel?" he asked. "When you stand in this atrium and are surrounded by beauty, what senses come to life?"

Beth couldn't argue. She'd always felt a strange oneness with wild things, not necessarily just wildlife, but the Earth itself—and something deeper. Something she'd never been able to give a name. At times she could swear that the forest, the trees, the flowers, the tall grass—all of it— almost took on the voice of women. A soothing, musical tone.

"You have a connection to our goddess that no others of our kind here have," Brad explained. "Your blood is special. You come from a long, long line of priestesses who've been able to physically travel to the space between this world and the next and directly communicate with the goddess.

"Long line of priestesses?" Beth looked over at her mother. "This is something you can do?"

"No, it has been seven generations since the ability has shown itself," Rena answered.

"So how do you know I can do this?"

"Your hair," Dane chimed in.

"My hair?" Beth almost laughed.

Dane continued. "You also carry the mark of the goddess."

"Mark?"

"On your right shoulder," he said.

Beth turned to look at the birthmark on her right shoulder. It was in the shape of two triangles forming a star.

"This?" she asked.

"Yes," Brad replied. "When you take your vows and eat from the tree of knowledge, you'll be the first to commune with our goddess in many, many years. And there are those who now live in darkness and serve a darker god who don't wish this to happen. They fear it will energize our cause."

"And what is that?" Beth asked him. Although she had a strange intuition that told her everything she was hearing was true, she had to admit she was somewhat scared at the same time. How could she not be?

"To protect the freedom of humans on this planet. When we first came here, there were some of us who felt we were superior to the life that was already here. They thought we should be able to decide the humans' fates and use them to our benefit."

"You mean make them slaves?" Beth asked.

"Yes, that's what I mean. Make them slaves and take their will."

"So when I talk to this goddess, the goddess, what am I supposed to say?"

"She'll tell you the destiny of our species. She'll guide you so that we may carry out her will," Brad continued.

"No pressure there," Beth said. "So when is the ceremony and what does it entail?

"It will be on your birthday, the first new moon of the year—the wolf moon. This moon symbolizes the removal of the bad and the welcoming of the good. It must be this moon," Rena answered.

Beth took in a deep breath. The weight of what she was hearing was starting to settle on her shoulders.

"When the moon rises to the highest point in the sky, you'll eat from the tree of knowledge, the very same tree that Eve herself ate from, and your soul will travel to the world between," Dane said. "What happens there is only for you to know. It's also at this point that you'll shift into the sacred animal you'll share form with. This animal will be like a companion that lives deep in your soul. It will guide you throughout your life, and you'll never feel alone again."

Up until this point, Dane had seemed more interested in the food on the table than the conversation.

"What's your animal, Dane?" Beth asked.

"I'm a guardian. Most guardians shift into cats, but not all," he answered.

"Like a house cat?" Beth looked confused.

Everyone at the table laughed, and suddenly a warm wind and bright light seemed to surround Dane, just like the one that had surrounded her mother before she shifted. Then, sitting before Beth was the largest mountain lion she'd ever seen. He made normal mountain lions look like kittens. He slowly walked over to Beth and began to purr while gently rubbing his head on her shoulder. Beth could easily recognize Dane's eyes. Then suddenly she heard him speak in her mind.

"Pretty cool, huh?"

"Yeah, way cool," she replied.

And with that, a warm wind moved and bright light once again shone. Now it was Dane standing in front of her.

"You said you're a guardian. What's that?" Beth asked.

"Think of it like a bodyguard. However, we swear to protect only a single person. I've taken my vows to protect you. As your guardian, I'll do so until my last breath."

Beth was silent. She couldn't believe Dane would spend the rest of his life protecting her. It almost didn't seem fair.

"So, how did you become my guardian?"

There was suddenly an awkward silence at the table, and Beth noticed nobody was making eye contact. Clearly this was a more personal subject that nobody wanted to discuss. But Beth could guess it had something to do with love and her mother.

"I took the vow because you're a special girl, Beth. Your soul is pure, and you're good through and through," Dane finally responded.

After the awkward silence had disappeared, Beth realized she now had a bowl of soup in front of her and Marco had cleared all the salad plates.

"Can I get anyone a refill?" Marco asked in a chipper voice that, at the moment, seemed out of place.

"I think we're fine, but thank you," Brad answered. And again Marco scurried off in the direction of the kitchen.

"So I eat this apple and go talk to our goddess. And then what?" Beth asked.

"And then we'll proceed accordingly," Brad said between spoonfuls of soup.

"OK, meaning what?" Beth was getting a bit irritated by his evasive answers.

Setting down his spoon, her father looked at her. "Those who have chosen to serve darkness will stop at nothing to achieve their goal. We must not allow this to happen."

"So we what? Go to war?"

"We're already at war." Her mother answered this time, just as Marco arrived again with four plates of steaming fish.

Beth stood to excuse herself. She was just about to turn eighteen, and now she was being told she was joining a war between good and evil—a real war. Again, she couldn't help but feel like she was suddenly in the middle of a teenage fantasy novel. "Would you mind if I went to lie down? I'm suddenly not feeling so great."

"No, not at all, honey. We'll save your lunch for you. You go and get some rest," her mother said.

Beth couldn't help but notice that Marco seemed rather disappointed that she wouldn't be eating the Alaskan halibut he was so very proud of.

"Thanks for all the food, Marco. It was great," Beth said, hoping this would ease his disappointment.

"My pleasure, Beth," he said, still clearly a bit dismayed. "I'll keep this warm for you to have after your nap."

"Thank you for your kindness," Beth replied. This seemed to lighten Marco's letdown.

And with that, Beth gave everyone a polite smile and excused herself. She needed to think, alone.

CHAPTER

NINE

Michael sat in the airport staring at the departure board while the world moved around him. He felt very detached from everything as he replayed his father's last moments over and over in his mind. He hadn't fully grasped yet what had happened. Why would someone want to hurt his father? Especially one of their own? He figured they must have cut the fence to separate him and his father and have time to attack.

I should have gone to help the minute I saw that bird, Michael thought. *If I'd gotten to him just a few seconds earlier, maybe Dad would still be alive.*

He felt as if he was an orphan. He didn't have much of a relationship with his mother even though she'd raised him in Billings. She was distant, and always had been. She never spoke of what they really were—almost as if she wanted to forget. This was a major part of the reason he loved the month he got to spend with his father. At least there he could shift as he pleased. Although Michael didn't get to see much of his father, he remembered the proud look on his father's face at his coming-of-age ceremony. His mother hadn't even attended and wasn't there when he'd shifted into a wolf for the first time. It was a moment etched in his mind. That was the first time he'd truly felt close to his father. His heart sank with the memory. Either way, he realized he was going to have to find a way to tell his mother at some point. Michael had no idea how she would take it. She never displayed much emotion when it came to his dad.

Suddenly pulled from his thoughts, Michael realized a woman was trying to get his attention.

"Sir, this is your boarding call," she said.

"Oh, thank you," Michael responded. Then he grabbed his bag and handed the women his ticket.

"Seat 3A, sir," she said.

Michael gave the flight attendant a quick smile and started to walk toward the plane. As he boarded, he noticed a gentleman in front of him wearing a white T-shirt. He was tall with a shaved head. Michael could see he was sleeved down on both arms with tattoos, but he was too far ahead for Michael to make out what they were. The gentleman proceeded all the way to the back of the plane, the total opposite from where Michael was seated at the front. As Michael placed his bag in the overhead compartment, he glanced toward the back of the plane again, this time making brief eye contact with the man. His eyes were green, very green.

He's one of us, Michael thought.

Picking up on the obvious recognition, the man waved and gave a small smile. Michael's heart started to pound. *Is this the guy? Is that man the one who killed my father?*

Michael sat down quickly and tried to calm himself. With less than a thousand purebred Annu on this planet, what were the odds that he and this man had both ended up on this flight? Michael looked around, seeing that the plane was filling up. He decided there was nothing he could do about it at this moment, so he pulled out some headphones and got ready to watch the in-flight movie.

Michael dozed off several times during the flight. Opening his eyes and stretching, he saw it was dark out. He realized they must be close. Just at that moment, Michael heard the captain on the overhead speaker.

"Well, folks, we want to say thank-you for flying with us today. We're starting our final descent into the windy city of Chicago. Please keep your seat belts fastened and your tray tables in their upright and locked position. And again, thank you for flying with us."

Michael once again glanced behind him, seeing the gentleman in the back of the plane. He now looked to be fast asleep. Michael squinted his eyes to try and make out the tattoo on his right forearm. *Is that an eagle?* he wondered. But it was just too far away. He would have to wait until the plane landed.

Michael had never been to Chicago before, but he imagined it was like any other city—overcrowded and loud. As much as he didn't want to admit it, he'd become much more of a cowboy in the last few years. He preferred the quiet life of a ranch to the hustle and bustle of the city.

Slowly, the passengers started to line up as they waited for the flight attendant to open the plane doors. Michael didn't care for airplanes. They made him claustrophobic, and he never really understood how they flew. They seemed like a giant tin can to him.

Finally the line started to move, but Michael waited until the gentleman from the back of the plane got closer so he could see his tattoo. A bear—it was a tattoo of a bear, not an eagle. Michael felt his body relax a bit, knowing he wasn't standing almost face-to-face with his father's killer.

Michael exited the plane and headed to the large food court in the airport. He had some calls to make to figure out where this ceremony was being held and where he'd be staying. He grabbed a table out of the way of all the people coming and going, then pulled out his phone.

"Mind if I sit?"

Michael looked up and saw the same gentleman from the plane. The one with the bear tattoo.

"No, go ahead. I'm Michael," he said, putting out his hand to shake the gentleman's hand.

"Eric," the man replied. "You headed to the ceremony for Rena's daughter?"

"Yes, actually. You?" Michael answered.

"Sure am. You want to ride together? I can show you the best hotel around here to stay in, and I've already got a rental car set up."

"Yeah, that sounds great," Michael said. "I was just about to start calling around to try and figure out where this thing is. So, you were coming from Montana as well?"

"Well, not really. It was cheaper to get a ticket with a layover in Montana than it was to fly straight through. I'm actually from Washington. Seattle, to be exact. "

"Do you know Rena and her daughter?"

"No, not personally, but I know the Annu have been waiting for this day to come for seven generations. I would imagine every single one of us on this planet will be there. Well, that is, those who haven't chosen to live in darkness."

Darkness. That's what murder was. Michael's grief came flooding back and hit him like a ton of bricks. He had to take a minute before he could speak again. He knew how much his father had been looking forward to Rena's daughter coming of age. He'd felt so privileged to live in a time when the true descendant of the goddess was living, and he'd always made sure Michael knew what a special thing it was. That's what Michael told himself to hold on to.

"Let's go grab that car and head to the hotel," Eric said, interrupting Michael's thoughts.

"Sure, sounds good," Michael replied, grabbing his bag.

"No luggage? Just the bag?" Eric asked while he picked up a large suitcase.

"I travel light," Michael said.

Michael followed Eric through the large airport and finally out to where the rental car place was. After standing in line for what felt like forever, they finally got into the car and headed downtown.

"I've spent a lot of time here. I can show you the best places to party," Eric said while driving. "You know, places that cater to our kind."

"I'm not much of a partier. What do you mean, 'places that cater to our kind?'" Michael asked.

"You know, places that let only the Annu in the door. They're great. There's always some kind of drama. You know, booze and shifting can be fun or dangerous." Eric laughed. "I'll have to take you to a fight. You like to bet?"

Michael thought about it for a second. That might be a good place to ask a few questions and see if he could get some information about his father—or at least find somebody willing to help. "Yeah, I could go for that," he finally said.

"Cool, man. Maybe this trip won't be so bad. What about a girlfriend? You got one of those?" Eric asked.

Michael got a little embarrassed about the question. Not only did he not have a girlfriend, he'd never even kissed a girl. Once, when he was nine, he'd kissed the neighbor girl at the local swimming pool. Even though they'd been underwater, she'd jumped out of the pool, started to cry, and took off running. "Nope, no girlfriend," he finally said.

"Well, we'll have to see if we can fix that. My girlfriend, Angie, will be flying in tomorrow. Maybe she has some friends we could hook you up with." Eric laughed while putting his hand up for a high five.

Michael didn't say anything. He just smiled and gave the guy a high five.

TEN

Beth slowly climbed the stairs back up toward the apartment, running her hand along the wall and feeling the texture of the wallpaper. She slowly went over the lunchtime conversation in her mind. Slaves? War? Crossing to speak with a goddess? Was this really happening to her?

Beth closed the door to the apartment behind her and pulled out her cell phone. Five missed calls and five text messages, all from Anna. Anna was the one person outside Beth's family she could talk to and never worry about being judged. The two had met when they were nine years old and had been best friends ever since. Anna came from a pretty broken home, and Beth had always had her mom and Dane, which she considered her family. Not to mention, Beth thought people always just assumed Dane was her father, considering he'd lived with them her entire life. In fact, Beth always considered her mother and Dane to be her complete family unit. So when it came to Anna, Beth had always tried to include her in as many family things as she could. She'd even tried to bring Anna on this trip, but

Anna still had six months of her senior year left, and Beth had managed to graduate half a year early.

Without reading the messages Beth dialed Anna's number. She answered on the first ring.

"OMG! Where have you been? What if your plane had crashed?"

Beth smiled at Anna's concern. "You would have heard about it on the news."

"So not funny."

"I'm fine. How are you? Loving school?"

"Please. Trying to get through English lit. And watching the Heathers do each other's hair and climb all over their boy toys makes it impossible to keep my breakfast down."

Beth laughed out loud. The Heathers were the popular group of girls that consisted of Heather Baker, Heather Ferring, and Heather Malik. They too had been inseparable since they were in grade school. One-on-one, they were OK, if you were ever lucky enough to catch one of them alone. But put the three of them together with their blonde hair and makeup, and they were a hurricane of mean.

"Well, it could be worse. You could actually be a Heather," Beth replied.

"I don't think my mom was sober enough to spell something much more difficult than *Anna* when I was born."

Anna joked a lot about the many mistakes her mother had made when she was younger, but deep down, Beth knew it hurt her—especially because she was still making those mistakes. The only difference now was that Anna was old enough to not have to be around it.

"Anyways, enough about this boring old place. How's your vacation! Man, I wish I was there."

So did Beth. She could really use a giant dose of Anna in

person. "It's good, you know?" Beth said. "Tall buildings with lots of people."

"What's wrong?" Anna asked in her serious tone—the one that always made it clear she would accept nothing but the truth while still keeping her tone light and cheery.

"Nothing. It's great." Beth didn't think it was a good idea to try and tell her anything about what was really going on—not to mention, Beth didn't think she could make any of it sound believable.

"Tall buildings? And lots of people? Girl, what's going on?" Anna asked. "You were so excited to go on this trip that you didn't shut up about it for weeks. And that's all you're going to say?"

"Really it's great. We're actually getting ready to go shopping," Beth fibbed, trying to sound more normal.

"If you say so," Anna said, making it clear she didn't believe her at all. "Well, I gotta get back to my homework. Promise you'll call again later tonight?"

"Promise. Love you."

"You too!" And with that, Anna disconnected the call.

Beth put the phone down and sat on the bed. She grabbed the TV remote, thinking maybe she could find something to drown out the noise in her head. Feeling her eyes get heavier while flipping through the channels, she realized she really was tired and decided to let herself fall asleep.

After what felt like just a split second, Beth opened her eyes, noticing they were extremely heavy—almost like she was waking up from a deep sleep. She looked around and immediately felt panicked. She wasn't sitting on her bed in the apartment. Instead, she was sitting on what looked like nothing and was surrounded by a super-thick fog. She jumped to her feet which made everything even stranger.

She was now standing on what could still be described only as nothing—the closest thing to oblivion Beth had ever seen.

"Hello!" Beth called out, rubbing her eyes.

"I'm asleep. This isn't real" she said to herself, but something told her that this wasn't a dream and she was awake.

"Hello!" she yelled again, able to feel the presence of somebody.

"Hello, love," she heard from somewhere in front of her. Beth jumped back, startled by the male voice. She held her breath, afraid to answer. Whoever it was sounded close.

"No need to be afraid," the voice said.

"Well, if that's the case, then why don't you show me who you are?"

With that, the space directly in front of her started to take on the shape of a man, who slowly came into view. He was about the same height as Beth, and his eyes were a beautiful chocolate brown. But they were so vibrant that they seemed to glow. He had long thick black hair and a perfectly chiseled body. The light behind him almost made it look like he had wings, and Beth immediately got the sense that he wasn't of the normal, material world.

"Is this better?" he asked with a warm smile.

"Yes," was all Beth was able to get out.

"You don't seem to recognize me," he said, sounding almost amused. "Has it really been so long?"

Beth was now thoroughly confused and becoming a little intimidated. "I'm sorry. Should I know who you are? Something tells me if we'd met, I would remember."

The gentleman let out a giant laugh, startling Beth and causing her to take another step back.

He took a step forward, keeping the gap between them small.

"I forget how much fun you can be."

Beth simply stood there with a blank stare.

"I'm just here to welcome you back," he said.

"Back? Where have I been?"

The man again smiled wide, showing his perfect white teeth, then clapped his hands just once. His form started to fade, and she heard him say, "I've missed you." And with that he was gone.

Beth found herself lying again on her bed in the apartment. She was totally alone, just as she'd originally been.

She flew off the bed and ran out the door, heading as fast as she could down the stairs and back to the atrium, where she'd left her family.

"MOM!" she yelled.

Hearing her daughter in distress, Rena jumped up from the table and ran to meet her. Beth looked truly scared and confused as she jumped into her mother's arms.

"What is it?" her mother frantically asked.

"I went somewhere. I saw someone. He was right there directly in front of me. I knew he was real, and it wasn't just a dream. He said, 'Welcome back,' or something weird like that." Beth stumbled over her words as she tried to describe her experience.

"What did he look like?" her mother asked with a very serious tone.

"He looked perfect—perfect, with brown eyes. He seemed familiar, but I can't put my finger on it. He said we'd met before."

"How's that possible?" Dane asked, looking at Brad.

"I don't know," Brad replied. "Did he say anything else, Beth?"

"No. Who is this guy? Can you please tell me what's going on?" Beth said, still reeling with fear but with a tinge of irritation in her voice.

Rena slowly walked Beth over to the table and pulled out a chair. Then she handed her a glass of water.

Beth, suddenly realizing how thirsty she was, took the glass and drank every drop. "Wow, I needed that."

"Your body is depleted from traveling," Brad said.

"Traveling?" Beth whispered, almost too afraid to ask.

"How did she travel before her ceremony? She hasn't eaten from the tree of knowledge," Rena said with a look of fear.

"OK, but who's the guy?" Beth asked for the second time.

"Think of him as an angel. Not a god, but more powerful than a humanoid being," Brad answered.

"More powerful than us?" Beth asked.

"In some ways, yes. But they're not bound by the light. They may serve darkness at any time. What they want or what their purpose is, it's never clear. I believe it was Gabriel you saw."

"Gabriel?"

"He's come and gone from history many times with many names. He tries to portray himself as a god so the people of Earth will follow him into the bonds of slavery. At least that's what we believe his goal is. But each time, he's rooted out by the light and disappears, sometimes for years."

"OK. Well, that doesn't explain what he wants with me," Beth said, trying to wrap her head around what she was hearing.

"He can only communicate with those who are descendants from the goddess herself, such as you. You've reincarnated many times over, just as we all have. But for you it's different, because if he can sway you to his cause, then the rest of us are lost. Each time you're born, he does his best to influence you. To put it plainly, you have a history with him," Beth's father answered.

Great, Beth thought. *Boy baggage from another life. This just gets better and better.*

ELEVEN

Michael grabbed his bag and quickly followed Eric across the street and into the hotel. *Clearly he has some money*, Michael thought. *This isn't the type of place the average traveler stays in if they're on a budget.*

"Do you mind sharing a room?" Eric asked, interrupting Michael's internal banter as they stood in front of the lobby desk after checking in.

"Nah, man, not at all. Here, let me pitch in."

"It's all good. Already paid for, courtesy of the McCarther estate."

"You know them? I mean, personally?"

"No, not me. My girlfriend does. Or at least her family does. I'm not really sure how it works, but I'm not complaining. No way could I afford this place for a night, let alone two weeks."

"Two weeks? What are we going to do for two weeks?"

"Well, the ceremony itself is in a few days, but there are a few parties we gotta go to before and after that. But really, we do whatever we want. Trust me, there are plenty of things we can do to stay busy. Tomorrow night after we pick up Angie from the airport, we head over to the McCarthers' place to formally meet Beth and her family. After that, we're free to party."

"You said something about fights?"

Eric lowered his voice so the gentleman at the counter couldn't overhear. "Yeah, watching shifters fight is great. Not only is it way entertaining, it's also a great way to make some money. Think of it like a boxing match. Have you ever seen an eagle fight? They're crazy, and nine times out of ten, they win. You wouldn't think they'd win against a wolf or a bear, but man, they hold their own."

Michael felt his stomach fall. He knew all too well that an eagle shifter could fight. He'd actually managed to go a few minutes without thinking about his father. He wondered if a time would ever come when he didn't feel this hole in his heart.

"You think we could go to a fight after this party tomorrow?" Michael asked. He couldn't think of any better place to start getting some info on who would want to hurt his father. Maybe somebody at this introduction dinner the next night could help.

"Yeah, I'll ask around. I'm sure we can find one. Want to grab a drink?" Eric asked as the two of them started toward the elevator to find their room.

"Actually, I'm pretty tired. Long day, man. I think I might just hit the sack."

"You're right," Eric said. "Plenty of time for that. I think I might just crash out too."

As they walked into their hotel room, Michael couldn't believe this was considered just one room. It had an actual living room and what looked like two separate bedrooms with king-size beds. *If the McCarthers are paying for this for two weeks, they must have some serious money*, Michael thought.

"Feel free to check out the minibar. And it looks like we have pay-per-view also," Eric said while messing with the TV remotes.

The living room had a giant flat-screen TV on the wall, along with a fireplace burning underneath it. Two sets of sliding doors opened up to the terrace, with a beautiful view of the city. They were eleven floors up, and it was amazing.

"Crazy that people live like this, isn't it?" Michael said, more to himself than anyone else. But still, Eric answered.

"Yeah, man. It must be nice, right? Me, as long as I got a surfboard, waves, and my girl, I'm happy. Angie and I don't spend a lot of time at our place in Seattle. We follow the waves around the world. I could have gone pro, but it's kind of forbidden for the Annu to compete in human sporting events. It's not exactly fair, with our superior physical abilities."

"How long have you two been together?" Michael asked.

"Forever. Like since sixth grade, no joke. She's great. You'll like her. And you? Why no girlfriend, man? Having trouble picking just one?" Eric laughed, obviously thinking he was funny.

Michael smiled. "Does your girl know everything about you? I mean, does she know where we come from and what we can do?"

"Is that what's stopping you from getting a girl, man? Yes, of course she knows. She's one of us as well. But even if she wasn't, I would still totally love her," Eric said with that dazed, "I'm in love" look. "You know a lot of the half-breeds can shift. They just don't know it."

"Really?" Michael asked in amazement.

"Yeah, totally. The gene is passed from the mother, so if the mother was a shifter and the father was human, that baby will still be able to shift if they were to eat from the tree of knowledge. But there are all kinds of red tape you gotta go through to get it approved. But who cares about all that if your mate can shift with you."

"How are you supposed to know if someone is part shifter if they don't even know? We all have some sort of streak in our hair, be it black or white. And along with our eyes, we're easy to pick out, especially if you see a tattoo."

"A lot of times, they'll have the same hair we do, or they may only have bright eyes. When you meet one, trust me. You'll know. They may not be 100 percent shifter, but they definitely carry themselves differently than humans. How do you not know any of this? It sounds like you're just finding out about what we are," Eric said in a joking tone. "But seriously, where have you been? It seems like this world is a bit new for you."

Michael became quiet and found a comfortable chair to sit on in their extremely large living room. Then he popped open a can of soda and small bottle of vodka from the minibar. "Just one drink," Michael said to Eric, with a question mark clearly on his face.

"Why not? Pour me one up too," Eric answered. "Got any more questions about our kind I can school you on?" This time he sounded a little more serious. "Or better yet, why don't you tell me what you do know, and I can fill in the blanks."

Eric suddenly lit up like he'd just had a flash of genius. "We can make it a drinking game!"

Michael laughed and smiled at how genuine Eric was. It was cool to meet people who didn't hide behind an invisible barrier, afraid to be judged. Eric lived in the moment, and it was great.

Michael held up his cup, which was filled with Coke and vodka. "I don't know how many of these I'll be having, but sure. Why not? Who starts, and how do we play this game?"

"Yes!" Eric jumped up and, in a hurried scramble, raided the minibar, bringing one of everything over to the coffee table, which sat between the couch and two chairs. Michael laughed at Eric's childlike energy level. He didn't sit still for long.

"OK, bro. This is how it will go. Each of us will make a statement about something or someone or anything that has to do with our history, Annu related or not, and if the other doesn't know what they're talking about, they take a drink!"

Eric clearly thought this game was masterly.

"I think I can live with that, but you go first," Michael said.

"No problemo. OK, let me think. Wait, I got it," Eric said while standing up like he was getting ready to teach a class. "Did you know we can shift only once we've gone through our ceremonies and have eaten from the tree of knowledge?"

Michael burst out laughing, leaving Eric looking a bit confused. Michael stood and said, "I thought this game was going to be hard. Of course I know that! So that means you drink first."

Eric picked up his glass and drank before speaking. "OK, I can see we're going to have to start asking more than just the basics. Have no fear. I'll be able to stump you."

Michael was really enjoying just hanging out and doing silly kid-like stuff, being in a place where not everything was so serious. Just chillin', as he imagined Eric would say.

"That may be, but it's my turn," Michael said.

"Bring it on," Eric replied, putting himself in a football linebacker-like stance. Bring it on."

"OK, did you know there are supposedly only a thousand of our kind still here?"

"What! No way, maybe a thousand purebreds, but what about all those who don't even know they're half-human, half-shifters? I say we both have to drink on that one."

"Yeah, you're probably right," Michael said. And with that, he grabbed a glass, clinked it against Eric's, and swallowed the whole thing down.

"Damn, boy! So much for only one drink," Eric said while pouring both of them another.

"OK, it's your turn, Eric."

"I do believe you're right. OK, I got one for you. Did you know only females can shift into eagles?"

Michael was shocked. He couldn't believe it. That would mean the person who'd killed his father was a woman. Why would a woman want to commit such a vile act?

Michael suddenly realized Eric was speaking. "Earth to Michael. Did you know that one, or do you gotta drink?"

Michael tried to recover from his momentary lapse of fun and joy, and return to the party scene. "Nope, didn't know that one. So guess I gotta drink." And with that, he pounded down another full glass.

"You know you can just sip it when we say drink, right?" Eric said in a kind voice that revealed a little concern.

"Of course I do. But hey, we're having a good night, so come on. Let's just keep playing."

"Your turn, boss man," Eric said while pretending to salute Michael.

Michael sat for a minute to think about what he actually knew about the Annu and where they'd come from. He'd learned a lot from his father over the single month each year when he'd get to see him, but other than that, it was just bits and pieces here and there he'd picked up on over the years.

"You gotta question, bro?" Eric asked, interrupting Michael's internal babbling.

"Did you know there's a story passed down from many, many generations ago by the Hopi people that the powder put into our tattoo ink from the meteorite that hit the Earth the same day we arrived could somehow give us the ability to open up portals? To where, I have no idea. But they say in certain places on the Earth, we could open them."

The room was quiet. It looked like Michael had stumped Eric on this one.

"Bro. Michael. Where did you hear that? Eric asked with almost a look of admiration.

"My father. My father, and his father before him, and so on never interbred with the humans on this planet. He said that would dilute our blood and we'd lose our connection to the goddess. He knew many things—things I'll never learn now because he's dead."

As soon as it came out of his mouth, Michael wished he hadn't said it. He knew he sounded hurt and deeply wounded, making it clear his father's death was recent. He didn't want people to know yet—not until he could get some answers.

Eric picked up all the minibar bottles and cups, then cleared the table. He could sense drinking time was over. After placing everything in the small kitchen sink, he put on some hot water for tea and a pot of coffee, not knowing which Michael preferred.

Michael was still sitting on the living room couch, just looking out the window and taking in the gorgeous view of the Chicago night sky, when Eric walked over with two cups—one with coffee and one with tea. Clearly, he wanted Michael to choose.

"I'll take tea, thanks," Michael said.

"No problem, brother. Anytime." Keeping the coffee for himself, Eric sat down next to Michael on the couch. "You want to talk about it?"

"About being able to open up a portal?" Michael asked, even though he knew full well what Eric had meant.

"How long ago?"

Michael knew this question was about his dad, not the portals. "Three days ago."

"Three days ago? Really? And you're here?" Eric said in a shocked voice.

"Wait, it gets better," Michael said. "Not only is he dead, but I watched a giant eagle come down from the sky and shred him to pieces with her talons. I was too slow to get to them. Whoever it was cut one of our cattle fences, knowing it would be me who went to round up the livestock that had wandered off. I was too far away. By the time I saw the bird in the sky and realized my father was in trouble, it was too late. I ran as fast as my legs could take me, but he'd been pierced in the heart."

There was just silence in the room for a while, or maybe just a few minutes, but it was clear Eric was no longer in a joking mood. He could see that Michael's heart was broken. Finally he spoke. "Your mother? Is she here?"

She's alive but really not a participant in this life, or any life for that matter."

"Murder among the Annu is never random. It's considered barbaric and not a line that's crossed easily.

"Eric, I know all of this."

"No, what I'm trying to say is, for something to happen, it must have been given as some kind of order from someone."

"But who? Where do you even start looking?"

"Well, Mikey, I think we're in the best spot we could be in to start, with this dinner party tomorrow night. Murder with us just doesn't happen. But if it does, it's my bet someone in that house will be able to give us some sort of lead."

Michael stood up and started to pace around the living room, all the while rubbing his hand through his thick hair.

"Why do you want to help me with this, Eric?" he asked. "I mean, we just met."

Eric walked over to where Michel was standing, held out his forearm with the giant bear tattoo, then grabbed Michael's forearm, where the giant image of a wolf was tattooed.

"This makes us brothers. We're all bound together in ways no human could ever understand." Then suddenly, Eric started to speak to Michael in his mind. "And this makes us brothers. We're all family, and when someone hurts a member of your family, you take it personal."

Michael gave Eric a giant bear hug to thank him. For the first time since his father was killed, Michael didn't feel alone.

TWELVE

Beth woke up in her extremely comfortable bed, grateful that nothing but sleep had happened after she returned to her room. No visits or traveling— just good old-fashioned black sleep. The sun was up, but she couldn't tell how high. *I guess it really doesn't matter what time it is. I'm supposed to be on vacation,* she thought.

"Mom!" she yelled, hoping Rena was just on the other side of the wall in her bedroom. Her door opened, and in walked her fully put-together mother.

"Yes, love?"

"You sure look nice. Are we going somewhere?"

"No, silly girl. Everyone is coming here to meet you this afternoon. I would have woken you up, but I thought that after yesterday, you might need a few extra winks of sleep.

"Wait. What people? How many people? And why would anyone want to meet me?"

"Honey, there will be hundreds of people who will come to partake in your coming-of-age ceremony. It's very important that all those involved understand their role in the ceremony."

"Their role?"

"Well, yes. Guardians, for example. Your security needs to be taken very seriously." Rena gave Beth a very stern look and said, "And that's not debatable at all. Your safety is the first and really only priority as far as I'm concerned."

"What time do I need to be ready then?" Beth asked just as her mother was opening the closet, which Beth hadn't realized was full of clothes. "Are those all for me?" she asked while jumping off the bed like a three-year-old going for a candy bar.

"Yes, of course they're for you. And if there's anything else you need, please let us know, and it will be handled," Brad said from the doorway.

Beth wasn't sure how long he'd been standing there, but she was sure she hadn't heard the door. He seemed to do that, kind of like Dane. He just showed up in strange places and at strange times.

"I'm sure there's more than enough here," Beth said while running her hand over all the wonderful material hanging in the closet.

"Rena, if I may please have a word," Brad said.

"Of course," Rena said, giving Beth a kiss on her forehead. "I'll be right back, honey. Look for something blue. You look so wonderful in blue."

Beth looked up at her father as her mother walked out of the room. He gave her a very warm smile before turning to follow Rena out the door.

"What's going on?" Rena asked the minute the door was shut. She knew Brad well, and she could tell something was off.

"Why would something be wrong?" he replied with a chuckle.

"Brad, don't play with me. I know you as well as I know myself, and you're up to something."

Smiling again, he grabbed Rena's hand and said, "Follow me."

They walked through the large house and toward the front door. Once outside, they headed toward a detached garage with three large doors. Pulling a garage door opener out of his pocket, he pushed the button, and the garage door to the far right started to slowly open.

"What is this, Brad? Why are we out here?" Rena asked.

"Because I would like to give my daughter a gift. But out of the utmost respect for her mother, I wanted to show you first."

The door finished opening, revealing a dark-blue BMW SUV.

"You bought her a BMW? Brad! You bought her a car!"

Brad burst out laughing. "Before you object, Rena, let me explain."

"I told you a long time ago that the only way she was going to make it in this world was if she didn't have access to your money."

"Our money, you mean," Brad said, taking a step closer to her and closing the gap between them. "Rena, I've done everything you've asked all of these years, no matter how it made me feel. But she's old enough to know the truth about many things now, and she's also old enough to decide for herself if she would like my help or not. She's the most amazing girl, and I never had any doubt that you'd do an amazing job. I also know you wanted her to have a normal upbringing, but you must remember now that she's not normal. The weight of the world may actually sit on her shoulders. So please let me finally spoil my daughter."

Rena looked from the car to Brad and took a deep

breath. She knew it was a small thing he was asking for after not being in Beth's life all those years. And she knew it would serve no purpose to tell him no.

"OK, but only because I hear they're extremely safe vehicles," she finally said.

Brad chuckled, then grabbed hold of her and kissed the top of her head. Rena's heart skipped a beat as he held on to her. She'd forgotten how good it felt to be in his embrace. She allowed herself to enjoy it for just a second, then pulled away, straightening her clothes while putting her emotions back in the little box she kept them in. When she turned to walk back toward the house, he spoke.

"Rena?"

"Yes." She stopped and turned around just as Brad hit the garage opener again, this time opening the second door and revealing a second car. It was identical to the first one, but this one was black.

"You didn't," she said.

"I need to know my girls are safe," he replied while placing a set of keys into her hands. Then he started to walk toward the house while calling over his shoulder, "I thought we would give it to her after dinner."

Rena just stood there with her mouth open, staring at her new BMW.

Back inside, Beth had taken out about half the clothes in her closet and was standing in front of a full-length mirror fastened to the back of the bathroom door. The gown she had on was a dark blue with spaghetti straps. It fit snug to her body down to her ankles, with a slit that went up the right side and stopped just above her knee.

"If you're going to wear that, you're going to need a shawl," Rena said from the door.

"Mom, I thought you were with Dad. I mean Brad. Besides, I'm old enough."

"Well, that's debatable," her mother answered.

"Not really. If it's in the closet, I'm old enough to wear it. All this stuff was for me, remember. What did he want?"

"Who?" Rena answered, seeming distracted.

"Who? Are you kidding me, Mom? What did Brad want?"

"Oh, nothing. He just wanted to go over seating."

"Seating?"

"Yes, seating."

"Whatever you say. Can you zip me up?" Beth asked while pointing to the back of her dress.

Rena walked over and slowly zipped up the beautiful blue dress that made her daughter's hair look as black as the night sky. She looked at Beth in the mirror, remembering when she was just a little girl and would stand on her little tippy-toes, holding her arms out, wanting to be held.

"I can't believe this day has come already," Rena said.

"Mom, I'm not getting married. We're just going to a party."

"No, not just a party. Tonight you'll choose your own guardians."

Beth turned around at lightning speed. "What do you mean? I don't even know these people. How am I supposed to choose anybody for a lifetime position?"

Rena could tell Beth was starting to panic. "How do you know Dane is a good man?" Rena asked.

"What? Because he is," Beth answered, shocked her mother would even ask such a question.

"But how do you know? What is it that tells you he's a good man? Is it because I told you? Or do you feel it? Before you answer, think about it. Every time you touch his hand or give him a hug, think about the feeling."

Beth sat down on the edge of the bed and closed her eyes. She knew her mother meant for her to really think about it. She slowly went over hugging him as a child, him throwing her in the air, and the joy that filled her heart. It was the same feeling she got every time she touched him. It had gotten stronger as she'd gotten older, but it had always been there. She thought about how safe that felt.

Rena could see her daughter's body relax as she went over things in her mind, and she knew she understood. "Do you see that feeling? It's almost tangible."

"Yes, I see what you mean."

"I know that feeling, that instinct, whether to trust or not, feels like it's second nature. But believe it or not, humans don't all have that ability. Or if they do, they don't know how to tap into it. That explains why they so often find themselves in dangerous positions with those who wish to do them harm. When you eat the apple, that feeling will become even stronger. You'll know if someone wishes you harm just by brushing against them."

"You can do this as well?" Beth asked.

"After we come of age and eat the apple, yes, we all can. But not like you. You're a direct descendant of our creator, Beth." She grabbed her daughter's hand and held on tight while continuing to talk. "You'll see and feel things that will elude the rest of us, and you must always trust yourself over others—even me."

"What do you mean 'even you'?" Beth tried to understand, but she couldn't fathom not trusting her mother.

"I mean no matter the question, after you eat the apple, you must always trust yourself first."

At that moment, there was a knock at the door,

breaking the intense stare held between Beth and her mother.

"Come in," Beth said, standing and straightening her dress.

"Look at you," Dane said with a giant smile as he walked in.

"You two act as if I'm getting married," Beth said, waving off her embarrassment.

"Well, this is just as important." Dane looked at Rena, a question clearly settling between them.

"What now?" Beth asked, looking from Dane to her mother.

Suddenly she heard her mother in her mind again. "He simply wants to make sure you're ready to choose tonight."

"OK. Until I can do the Vulcan mind meld thing too, let's stick with using our mouths to speak."

The three of them burst out laughing, mostly out of nervousness, but with an unsaid bond between them. Beth's heart swelled as she thought about the many happy years she'd had with just the three of them, their own little family, and she suddenly understood why her mother had kept this whole new world from her. She wanted her to have that—the sense of family without worry—and she was suddenly very grateful.

CHAPTER

THIRTEEN

Brad walked to the back of the house toward his study, pulling out a set of keys he always kept on him. He unlocked the heavy oak door, then closed it behind him. He simply stood for a moment and leaned against the closed door, taking in the familiar smell of cigars and lavender. It was a comfort. Lavender, Rena's favorite scent. It was funny—no matter how many times they reincarnated, she always loved lavender. She said its calming effect stayed with her soul.

Beth being there was easier than he'd anticipated. It was strange to know her so well, maybe even better than she knew herself at times. But for her to have no recollection of their relationship stung in a way. It was a small feeling, but it was there. He wondered why she couldn't remember her past lives like the rest of them could. There didn't seem to be much rhyme or reason to it—at least nothing he could put together that would explain it. He remembered when she'd been a baby this time. It had felt different. There was something that felt final, and clearly something was different. He wondered how she was able to travel or communicate with those beyond the veil before her ceremony. Whatever the reason, he had to make sure her security was beyond impenetrable. Nothing could be left to chance.

Brad pulled out his cell phone, noticing the time before he dialed his voice mail. People would be arriving soon, and he'd been so busy with the security detail that he hadn't noticed three missed calls and three voice mails from Trevor, one of the guardians in charge of the western district. The Earth was divided up into four districts, and Brad had four top guardians—one in charge of each district. The Americas were in the western district and made up the largest of the four.

"Brad, you need to call me," Trevor's message said. "Something has happened. I'm worried about the ceremony for Beth. Please call me as soon as you get this."

Walking over to his large desk and taking a seat in the oversized chair behind it, Brad sighed and deleted the message. He didn't listen to the two remaining. Instead, he dialed Trevor immediately.

"I know you're busy, sir, and I'm sorry to interrupt," Trevor said as soon as the call connected.

"It's alright. What is it?" Brad asked. He didn't like the sound of Trevor's voice. Not much shook the guy, but he sounded upset.

"We've had a death, caused by one of our own."

Brad was quiet for a minute before he answered. This wasn't what he wanted to hear, nor did he think the timing could be coincidental.

"Who was it?"

"Michael Bailey Sr. He owned a ranch up in Montana. He was responsible for our mining outfit down in the four corners. Looks like it was an eagle. Not just any eagle either.

This one had some training. The attack couldn't have lasted more than a minute or so."

"If I remember correctly, he has a son. Just about of age?"

"Yes, sir. He's actually on his way to your house now. Full-blooded wolf."

"Old enough to be a guardian?"

"Yes, sir."

"Any chance this kid was involved?"

"I wouldn't think so," Trevor replied. "Sounds like he put up a hell of a fight."

"We need to think about who's going to replace Mr. Bailey at the mine. I don't need to remind you how important that position is."

"I'll start working on it right away."

"No, I have someone in mind. I'll talk with her this evening," Brad said.

"Her? Sir, is that wise?"

"I'm sorry. I didn't realize you were in a position to question me and my decisions."

"No, sir. I apologize. Whoever you think is best. I didn't mean to. Again, sir, I apologize."

"Wait for my call." And with that, Brad disconnected. He had a lot of faith in Trevor's abilities to do his job, but he didn't like to be second-guessed on anything. That was probably the main reason Rena had decided to leave all those years ago. Brad had always thought Dane was the reason she'd left, but if he was really honest with himself, painstakingly honest, Brad knew better. She'd left because of him and no other reason. He wondered if anything over the years had developed between Rena and Dane. They seemed close, but if their relationship went any further than that, they were keeping it well hidden.

Almost on cue, Brad heard a knock at his door. "Come in," he said, sitting up straight again.

It was Dane, looking rather hesitant to step inside the room. "I'm sorry to disturb you," he said. "But I had some questions regarding security this afternoon."

"No, it's fine," Brad replied. "As a guardian, I would expect you to want to be involved."

With that, Dane stepped inside, closed the door behind him, and walked over to the chair directly in front of Brad's large oak desk.

"Well, first I was wondering what accommodations have been made for everyone arriving," Dane said. "Will everyone be at the same hotel?"

"Yes, I rented out a sizable portion of the Marriott downtown."

The two men sat in an uncomfortable silence before Dane spoke again. It had been many years since the two of them had been alone together. "Well, that was smart. How big is the pool of individuals who might be chosen as guardian? Have we run background checks on everyone?"

"Detailed information has been collected on everyone coming to the ceremony. No one will get close to her if we're not 100 percent sure they're on our side. But ultimately, the decision is hers. We have no control over that."

"I realize that, but as her guardian, I have to work with these people. And I want to make sure that anyone who could possibly be that close to her has been thoroughly vetted."

"I can promise you that's the case."

Again the room returned to that uncomfortable silence.

"Is that all then? Or is there something else we need to discuss?" Brad asked.

"Rena is vulnerable right now. I just wanted to make

sure you were being ..." Dane hesitated, trying to find the right words. "Careful with her."

"Dane." Brad sat up even straighter in his chair and leaned forward on his desk. "Rena doesn't need anyone to be careful, as you say, with her. She's probably the strongest woman I know."

Dane also sat up straighter and leaned forward on the desk, making it clear he wasn't going to be intimidated by Brad. It was almost as if he was responding to a silent challenge.

"With all due respect, Brad, Rena has always been somewhat fragile when it comes to you. I just want to make sure you realize she's having a difficult time letting go of Beth and that you tread carefully with her feelings."

Brad sat quietly for moment before answering. "As heartfelt as your concern is, Dane, I would appreciate it if you kept your attention on what's truly important and what's your business. And that would be the protection of my daughter."

Dane stood up, feeling the room go from uncomfortable to mildly hostile, then walked toward the door. He turned around just before he opened it.

"Brad, it's taken a long time for her to put herself back together. All I'm asking is that you know what you want before there are any misunderstandings." Dane opened the door and didn't give Brad the chance to respond before leaving the room.

Brad took a deep breath as the door shut. He closed his eyes. It was impossible to stop the memories from flooding back. He'd always known Rena would get pregnant. They'd been together for many different lifetimes. He could remember their deep commitment from life to life. It wasn't a memory, like going to the park or something routine like that. It was like a thread he could feel deeply. He and Rena were connected, and shadows constantly appeared, reminding him of the connection. Humans called it déjà vu.

When Brad had met Rena, it was like coming home. And when they'd had their first date, there was a deep sense they'd had many first dates—that he'd heard that wonderful laugh and seen that gorgeous smile time and time again. But things had changed once Rena got pregnant with Beth. Brad had truly been over the moon and filled with a joy deep in every bone in his body. But there was also deep sadness that overtook him. He was no fool. He knew Beth's safety was the only thing that mattered and that she had to have a guardian present with her at all time once she was born. At the time it was already clear that, due to certain events, darkness had begun to stir and certain members of their kind had been compromised by that darkness. Rena wanted Beth to have a normal life. She didn't want the privilege—or the danger—that came with being a member of the McCarther family, which had become very wealthy due to diamonds. The asteroid the family mined deep in the Earth's crust—the asteroid that had hit the Earth the day the Annu landed—was filled with some of the most beautiful diamonds this world had ever seen, along with other very important substances that humans didn't yet know the great value of.

It also helped that the family lineage went back thousands of years. They'd been on Earth since people simply traded goods for goods. They'd been a part of the first monetary systems—which many of their kind were against. Many of their kind felt the system promoted greed at its worst, but that was one of the ways those who served the dark were able to control the human race. Sure, there had been times in the beginning, when they'd first arrived on Earth, when humans were used for labor and treated like animals. That was before the great flood that was written about in their Bible. But some members had realized that if they could enslave humans without them knowing and without actual violence, it yielded much better results. Hence the invention of money. Humans could now be bought, and that type of slavery was very effective. Control the money, control the people. Other members didn't agree with this type of control. They didn't believe they should enslave humans to their cause to begin with, whatever that might be. Humans had their own evolutionary path to follow. Some of the Annu believed they didn't have the right to interfere. And that was the argument that divided them.

Those who served the dark had made it impossible for humans, or anyone else, to function in this world without money. The darkness had won that battle. The history of this world was now littered with stories of horrendous atrocities that stemmed from pure and simple greed. The human race was very vulnerable to emotions. They lacked the ability to make decisions without emotion. Even those who spoke the language of science—who thought they knew how to put emotion aside—truly couldn't see that it drove every decision.

But there was hope for them, and that was what many of the Annu held on to.

Either way, this is their world. We were the visitors, and we changed the course of history for them—we and our goddess. Brad rolled this thought around in his mind over and over, and as much as he would have liked to have simply stayed in his chair with the door closed in his own little world, he couldn't. People would be arriving soon. Whether she knew it or not, Beth's world would be changing, and he had to be there for her.

With that, Brad stood up, straightened his suit, and resigned himself to the fact that things were changing. This was the day he'd awaited for such a long time.

Then he walked out of his study.

CHAPTER

FOURTEEN

Michael opened the Jeep's passenger door and jumped in. He was nervous and didn't really know why. Someone might be able to help him figure out what had happened to his dad and why, but something else was bothering him—something he just couldn't put his finger on. He felt as if he was suddenly being pulled toward this event.

He looked around. *What's Eric doing?* he wondered. His new friend had been right behind him, and now he seemed to be nowhere. Michael was sitting in the hotel parking lot waiting on him; he wanted to get going. He didn't want to be last one showing up to this thing.

Suddenly, the driver's door opened and Eric jumped in. "Ready to go, man?" he said.

"Been ready," Michael responded in somewhat of an irritated voice.

"OK. Why so edgy, dude?"

"Sorry, I really am. I don't know. I just really want to get to this place, I guess."

"That makes sense. Don't stress. I promise you we'll get some answers," Eric said.

"It's not even that. I mean it is, and it isn't. Are you nervous about meeting this girl?"

"I'm nervous about being late to pick up Angie," Eric joked. Then he said, "Nah, man. I'm not nervous. Whatever our peeps have going on hopefully has nothing to do with us. We show up, watch her ceremony, party it up, and leave."

"Why do we have to go to this thing before the ceremony anyway?"

"Man, where have you been? You really know nothing about us, do you?" Eric asked in a more serious tone.

"No. I mean, I know things. I guess my dad figured we had plenty of time. He was really looking forward to this ceremony. But you're right. He took all of this so seriously, but he didn't seem to pass on very much, did he?" Michael watched the city pass by through the window. *All these people, each one on their way to something, and every one of them feels like their existence is at the middle of everything.* Michael suddenly felt very small.

"It's all good. I'll do what I can to fill in the blanks," Eric said. "We go to this thing before the ceremony so we can be introduced to Beth and shake her hand."

"What? This is all about saying hello?"

Eric started to laugh. "No, there's a bit more to it than just saying hi. When you're introduced, you'll shake her hand. And if you're one of the lucky ones, she'll choose you as her guardian. "

"What?" Michael asked, almost snapping.

"What do you mean?" Eric was confused by Michael's sharp tone.

"You mean, we could possibly end up pledging our lives to her?"

"It's not quite like that. When you shake her hand, if you're bound to her, you'll know, and you'll want to pledge your life to her. These are bonds that go back lifetimes. Nothing is more sacred than the bond with a guardian. How do you not know this?" Eric asked almost with a laugh.

"I don't know. These are things my father should have told me." Michael was really starting to feel stressed, but at the same time, there was a small amount of excitement that he didn't want to acknowledge.

"Look, there are going to be hundreds of people there. Think of it like the lottery. You have virtually no chance of being chosen."

Michael rolled his eyes and laughed. He was grateful to have met Eric. His constant glass-half-full attitude was comforting.

As they pulled up to the airport, Michael could see a beautiful blonde girl standing on the sidewalk with several pieces of luggage. She was looking around and checking her phone as if she was waiting for someone and they were late. She didn't look irritated. If anything, she looked scared. Immediately Michael noticed the full-arm-length tattoo that started at her shoulder. It was an eagle with what looked like vines wrapping around its outstretched wings. It drew the eye right away.

"There's my girl!" Eric had a giant grin. It was clear he was very smitten with the girl. "Angie!" he yelled while honking the horn. "Over here, babe!"

Angie lit up like a Christmas tree the minute she saw them. Well, the minute she saw Eric, who pulled over and jumped out of the Jeep to greet her.

"Babe, I know we don't feel the cold, but really. A tank top looks strange in the middle of the winter," Eric said while picking her up and twirling her around.

"Maybe I just came from someplace tropical," Angie replied. "Besides, who cares what people think."

While Eric was busy hugging and kissing his girlfriend hello with their loving back-and-forth banter, Michael took it upon himself to get out, grab her bags, and throw them in the back of the Jeep.

"Thanks! You must be Michael," Angie said while sticking her hand out to shake his. Again, he took a moment to look at her tattoo. This was the first female shifter he'd met other than his mother.

"Nice tattoo," Michael said. "I didn't realize color was used on any of them."

"Some women's tattoos are in color, unlike men's," Angie said. She smiled while looking over at Eric with a clear question on her face.

"Oh yeah, Michael doesn't seem to know a whole lot about us, even though he's one of us."

"It's cool. We'll teach him," Angie said, laughing. "Nice hair. Eric doesn't let his grow." She ruffled Michael's hair in a playful sort of way.

"Babe, it gets in the way when I surf," Eric said, feigning hurt feelings.

The three of them laughed. There was a sense of familiarity among them, like they'd been best friends all their lives.

"Excuse me, there's no parking here," said a short man in a police uniform, who seemed to come out of nowhere.

"Yeah, yeah, we're leaving," Eric responded in a respectful tone, sounding only slightly irritated.

"We better hurry. First lesson," Angie said. "Shifters are never late."

Eric picked Angie up and threw her gently into the back of the Jeep. Then he gave her another kiss before he closed the door.

Michael smiled. It was clear she was just as into Eric as he was into her. Jumping into the driver's seat, Eric waved goodbye to the clearly perturbed policeman directing traffic.

The three of them joked and laughed the whole way to the house, making the time fly by. Before Michael knew it, the forty-five-minute drive was over and they were pulling into the driveway of the largest house in the area—definitely the largest house he'd ever seen.

As they pulled up, Michael could see what looked like a line of people outside waiting to get in. The three of them jumped out of the Jeep when the valet came up to the driver's-side door.

He imagined this was where everyone met Beth. Most of the women had sleeveless dresses on, all showing their tattoos. It looked like most females had an eagle tattoo. However, some had wildcats, and he saw only one female with a wolf tattoo. The woman smiled and nodded at him with an unsaid understanding. Michael would have given anything to be able to shift right there. He was so much more comfortable in his wolf form than he ever was as a human. He also realized that the three of them were seriously underdressed, which added to his anxiety.

"Bro, why didn't you tell me we needed to dress up?" Michael quietly said to Eric.

"It's all good, bro. Remember, we're only here to say hello."

"Don't worry. She's our age. She'll totally understand.

Besides, this isn't the actual ceremony," Angie whispered back.

The line didn't seem to be moving very quickly. *If the whole evening goes at this pace, we won't be leaving for quite some time,* Michael thought.

Looking up, he suddenly saw a man in a pinstripe suit with hair almost identical to his coming toward him. He walked with an air of confidence that Michael couldn't imagine having—the kind of confidence that comes only from knowledge.

"Michael?" the gentleman said, putting his hand out and making it clear this was some sort of introduction. But Michael had no idea who this guy was. Hesitantly, he took the man's hand and shook it.

"Uh, yes?" he answered, making his confusion clear with his tone of voice.

"My name's Brad. Brad McCarther."

Michael tried to keep his emotions in check, but if he had to guess, he would have said this was the father of Beth McCarther. *But if that's the case,* he wondered, *why in the world did he walk up to me in the middle of what has to be a hundred people still in line waiting to greet Beth and introduce himself?*

"I was sorry to hear about your father. Please find me after you've met my daughter, and we'll talk."

Michael was so shocked that he didn't respond. He just stood there looking exactly that—shocked.

As Brad walked off, Eric hit Michael in the shoulder and said, "I thought you said you didn't know these people."

"I don't. How does he already know about my dad?"

"What happened to your dad? I'm lost," Angie interjected. Finally the line seemed to be moving.

"He died four days ago," Michael answered.

"What?" Angie said, a little too loudly and causing the people in front of them to turn and look. She just smiled, slightly embarrassed. "I'm sorry. Did you say he died?" she asked, this time much more quietly. "How?"

Leaning over, Michael discreetly whispered in her ear, "An eagle attacked him on our ranch."

"What?" Angie said, again way too loud. "Sorry. I mean, What?" she whispered. "If this just happened, how does this Brad guy know about it? Who's your dad?"

"I don't know how he knows, but I intend to find out," Michael said.

The line now had finally moved to where the three of them could see Beth and what they assumed was her mother at the door. The minute Michael saw her, his jaw about hit the ground. Her hair was as black as the night sky, and her eyes were emerald green with a light behind them that drew him in immediately. His heart started to pound, and he hadn't noticed that Eric had been talking to him. Suddenly he was in front of Beth, looking at her tiny hand outstretched with the intention of shaking his.

"Hello, it's nice to meet you. I'm Beth McCarther."

"I'm Michael," he said, barely able get the words out. Then he finally took her small hand in his.

The minute he did, his life changed forever.

CHAPTER

FIFTEEN

Not long before she met Michael, Beth's feet had started to ache from how long she'd been standing there. She figured she must have shaken two hundred different sets of hands already. But whatever feeling she was waiting for definitely hadn't happened yet. Person after person with the most beautiful tattoos had come up to her. Beth truly felt like a country girl in comparison to them—especially the women. They reminded her of the gorgeous pinup girls in the tattoo magazines—the classy ones who looked like they came from money. Theirs was a different world than most lived in. They were airbrushed to perfection.

With a smile plastered to her face, Beth leaned over to whisper in her mother's ear.

"So, what exactly am I waiting for?" she asked as another group of people approached to introduce themselves.

"You'll know," her mother quietly replied while shaking the hand of a young woman and kissing the cheeks of someone Beth assumed was the girl's mother. Each had the beautiful image of a wildcat tattooed on her left arm.

"My daughter, Beth," Rena said while motioning for Beth to shake the girl's hand. Beth started to speak while taking the girl's hand but was abruptly cut off by the sensation of electricity shooting through her arm and into her entire body, causing her fingers to tightly grip the girl's hand.

"Hi, Beth. My name is Kia," the girl said, clearly picking up on the connection and the fact that Beth was having trouble speaking. "It's an honor to finally meet you, and it will be an honor to serve you." With that, Kia was able to pull her hand away.

"Thank you, you too," Beth managed to mumble.

"It felt like I couldn't let go," she told her mother, still in total awe over what had just happened. She knew that girl. She'd never met her, but she knew that girl. She knew her favorite color was blue, dark blue. She knew she spent a lot of time alone and had a hard time trusting people. She knew honesty was the most important trait she looked for in the few friends she had. She also knew she could trust this girl with her life.

"Well, one down," her mother said happily.

"That was intense," Beth said, not even realizing she'd been introduced to three other people since shaking Kia's hand.

"Everything about your life is intense, love," her father said, suddenly appearing next to her. "But now that you know what you're looking for, it should go a little quicker." He smiled and leaned down, kissing her forehead. "Your mother and I have something for you after dinner."

"Oh, really?" Beth said, lighting up at the thought of a

surprise. Brad smiled, enjoying being able to see a spark of happiness in his daughter's bright-green eyes.

"Excuse me," he suddenly said, looking as if he recognized someone. Then he walked toward a small group of three still in line to meet Beth. She tried to keep an eye on him, but it was impossible with a new group of people suddenly in front of her.

"Hi, I'm Beth. It's nice to meet you," she said yet again. She swore that after this, there wasn't going to be anyone left in this city whose hand she hadn't shaken.

People continued to greet her. Then, one by one, they went into the large house and out to the gardens, where they sat under large tents and waited for the food to be served. Beth noticed that Dane and her father were now nowhere to be seen, but she continued to stand alongside her mother and do her duty.

Just as she was about to say something to her mother, there was a strange, very underdressed boy standing in front of her. He looked a little shell-shocked. Beth couldn't help but smile. He looked exactly how she felt. His hair was thick and black, just like hers, and he had the noticeable white streak directly in front of his very blue eyes—blue eyes that seemed very familiar. Before he even took her hand, Beth knew what was about to happen. She put her hand out and said, "Hello, it's nice to meet you. I'm Beth McCarther."

The minute he put his hand out to grab hers, she swore she saw sparks fly between their hands—literal, actual sparks. Her fingers instantly gripped his hand as a whirlwind of images and feelings took over her. For just a moment, it was as if they were the only two people—not just in this large gathering of her kind, but in the world. In her mind's eye she saw him as a baby, then two or three years old. Suddenly he was grown and smiling at her. They were laughing together. Next she saw him as an aged man, and again he was smiling. The memories kept coming one after the other, from infancy to adulthood, over and over until suddenly it was quiet. Beth looked from Michael to the two people standing next to him. Both of them had stunned looks on their faces. It was then she realized the underdressed boy was speaking.

"I'm Michael—"

Beth cut him off. "Mom, I don't need to meet anyone else."

She had a lot to say to him but no words to say it, she realized. She knew she'd been waiting her whole life for this moment. Every choice she'd made, every word she'd spoken was to bring her here. Momentarily turning her attention back to his companions, she realized she knew them too. She didn't know how. She hadn't touched them, but she knew her search for guardians was over.

Her mother leaned over and introduced herself to the three very stunned-looking individuals. "Hello, my name is Rena. I'm Beth's mother, and you three, I assume, are her new guardians."

"Um, I'm Eric and this Ang, I mean Angie." Before he could finish speaking, Beth had scooped them up into a giant bear hug, and the minute she touched the two of them, there was no ignoring the electric pull. She knew them, and they knew her. It was like suddenly having a new family. The four of them just stood there not talking but knowing the importance of this moment. It was like coming home after being lost. These were bonds not even time could break.

"Why don't we all head to the gardens?" Rena spoke up, breaking the long silence.

"That sounds great, ma'am," Michael answered while grabbing Beth's hand. Then they started toward the back of the house. Part of him was afraid she would disappear. He was overwhelmed by the feeling that he couldn't let her out of his sight. But at the same time, he felt like something was still missing.

"I knew it, I just knew it," Angie said as she and Eric followed Michael and Beth. "This is why he didn't have a girlfriend." Angie giggled like a schoolgirl as they walked through the house and out to the back patio and gardens.

Beth had forgotten there were over two hundred people out there, and she suddenly became very nervous. *Do I have to speak?* she wondered. She hadn't asked her mother—or her father, who was standing at the front of the crowd with a giant smile. Then, as if to answer her question and in a voice that demanded attention, her father introduced the group.

"Ladies and gentlemen, I welcome you to our home for this very momentous occasion, and I introduce to you Beth McCarther and her guardians!"

The crowd erupted into cheers while the four walked to the front of the group. Beth looked around as if she'd lost somebody, then seemed to spot her immediately—a petite platinum-blonde girl with a giant tattoo of a wildcat on her forearm, who joined the group. Somehow Michael recognized her right away, and he watched as Beth scooped Kia up into a bear hug that rivaled the one she'd given him, Eric, and Angie earlier.

The five now joined hands, feeling the electricity surge between them. It was as if a thirst had been quenched or a hole they hadn't even known was there was now suddenly filled.

In the rear of the crowd, Beth could see her mother now

holding Dane's hand. She had a giant smile and what looked like tears in her eyes. Finding her father, she could see he'd also noticed the closeness that emanated between the two. It tugged at Beth's heart. She felt for her father. She knew there were things she wasn't aware of and that there was a good reason he'd been absent from her life. And although she couldn't imagine what those reasons were, she could see the love in his eyes—love for her and love for her mother. It was clear he would go to the ends of the Earth for them.

As the food was served, Beth chuckled as Marco ran around like a chicken with its head cut off, trying to make sure all two hundred people were served and getting what they needed. She knew he was probably all tied up in knots right now, and she had a twinge of guilt that this was all for her.

She looked at each of her guardians, knowing their souls but not knowing them as individuals in this life. And she wanted to know. She wanted to know about their families, where they lived, and what they'd been doing. This world was new to her, but to not them. They'd always known about the hidden existence of a whole other realm. It was amazing to her that she was in a place where over two hundred people, not natives of this planet, were able to morph into animals. It really was an incredible thing, and she knew it was just the tip of the iceberg. She was suddenly overwhelmed with a mountain of questions, but for now, they could wait.

She sat back and just took in the scene, capturing it in her mind. These were her people. And she knew that although she didn't know how or why, it was up to her to keep them safe. They were all so lucky to be here and to have found a new home on this Earth. But it wasn't only theirs, and she was taken aback by a fierce feeling. They were guests here on this planet, and they needed to remember that there'd been a whole evolution happening here before they arrived.

Then, for the first time, Beth heard a voice in her mind —a voice she knew belonged to their goddess.

"It begins," the voice said. "This won't be easy, but you'll be ready. I'm always here with you."

Beth only briefly wondered if she was losing her mind, but that thought brought out an actual laugh. That would be the easy answer, but this wasn't a figment of her imagination. This was really happening.

She felt a sense of calm overcome her. She didn't share what she'd just heard. She just held it close to her heart.

Her life had changed today, but this was only the beginning.

CHAPTER
SIXTEEN

The rest of the evening went fairly smoothly. Poor Marco, however, probably thought the opposite. More than a few times, Beth had seen him running frantically around, trying to keep up with the dinner crowd and its needs.

As they ate, from time to time, Beth saw a flash of light or heard the swoosh of the wind and saw someone change form. Each and every time someone shifted, she was amazed at how beautiful they were individually. But there was a definite sense of power that was impossible to ignore. It was the type of beauty she saw in wild animals—but always there was an awareness that the animal could over-power her. Over and over Beth thought about the day when she herself would be able to shift. That day was coming soon.

As the dinner wound down and people started to mingle, Brad brought their attention back to himself at the front of the crowd.

"As you all know, we're here for my daughter Beth—a dress rehearsal for the day she'll eat the apple and take on the form of whatever animal our goddess has paired her with. She'll also be the first in generations to commune with our goddess!"

As soon as the words left his mouth, the entire crowd erupted in cheers. Beth's cheeks turned bright red, as the focus was suddenly back on her. But her father kept speaking, and she was off the hook for the moment.

"Not that our needs in this world are physical, but it's known that to navigate this wonderful planet, certain things are needed." With that, he pulled a set of keys out of his pocket and walked toward Beth. He lightly grabbed her hand and set the keys in her palm with the BMW emblem faceup. She was absolutely speechless.

Is he giving me a car? she wondered.

"So you can explore and see the world. Safely," her father finished. Then Beth gave him the first real father-daughter hug they'd ever shared. She felt overwhelmed by the feelings of love that came from a man she'd just met a few days prior. Deep down, she didn't want to disappoint him, but she was nervous. She didn't know what eating the apple entailed. She assumed that before the actual event, they would go over it with her. But with all these people, here waiting on her for some divine instruction, she felt like a kid who was just learning to walk with no surety in her footing.

"Thank you, Brad," Beth said. "Can we go see it?"

"Of course," he responded.

And with that, Beth and her four guardians went back through the house and out to the garages. This would be the first time the five of them were alone.

As the garage door opened and they saw the car, all five mouths dropped.

"This is so awesome. You have the best dad ever," Eric

said, immediately opening the driver's-side door. "Angie, check this out. It's got an amazing GPS system in here, not to mention the music you can blast."

Angie walked around to the passenger door and grabbed Kia by the arm, leaving Beth and Michael alone.

Michael, looking nervous like a kindergartner on the first day of school, was the first to speak. "You know, your dad asked me to find him after I met you. I wonder if he knew about the guardian thing."

Beth smiled before answering. "Maybe he knew. I don't see how, but maybe. Did he say why he wanted you to find him?"

"No, but he gave his condolences regarding my father, so maybe it's about that."

Beth had a sudden pang in her heart. She knew the answer to the question she was about to ask was going to be sad. "What happened with your father?"

"He passed away last week."

Beth wasn't able to hide her shock as she heard those words. She reached out, putting her hand on Michael's shoulder. "I'm so sorry. Was it expected?" she asked, taking a step closer.

"No, one of our kind killed him. We were getting ready to come here for your ceremony."

Beth took a sharp breath in, although she knew he hadn't been killed because he was leaving to come here. At least she prayed it wasn't related. She didn't want to be the cause of anyone's pain—especially Michael's. She now took yet another step closer and took his hand in hers before speaking.

"Let's talk to my father. Maybe he can help."

And just like that, her father appeared, walking toward them from the house. As if he knew what they were talking about, he wasted no time with a hello. Instead, he addressed the topic directly.

"Michael, I can't tell you at this moment who killed your father, but I can tell you that will change. We will find out who did this. Were you aware of what your father did for the organization?" That was how Brad referred to the business side of things for their kind: the organization.

Looking somewhat confused, Michael answered, "No, sir. I thought he was just a rancher."

"No one is ever just a rancher. Or just a father. Yes, your father took care of his ranch. But his main job was security at our mine."

"Mine? What do you mean by *mine*?" Beth asked Brad, feeling like she was always one step behind.

"When our people landed, they were fortunate to have the location of a very large piece of space rock, an asteroid, that impacted the Earth right before their eyes. Once the weather stabilized and the water receded from the initial impact, we were able to locate it and start to mine what was left. Diamonds and things of that nature. But we also mine an element not found anywhere else on Earth. Most importantly, it's the element that makes it possible for us to shift."

This was news not only to Beth but also Michael. Why had his father kept so much from him? Especially so much about their history. He couldn't fathom what reason his father could have possibly had, and it slightly angered him.

"Wait. Could normal humans shift if they knew about this element?" Michel asked, clearly picking up the seriousness of Brad's tone.

"Honestly, I don't know. But it's possible, I suppose," Brad answered. At this point Eric, Angie, and Kia had joined the conversation. "My concern also circles around a few of our kind."

This definitely got the attention of the four guardians, who were now listening intently to Brad. "There are some who think we should have much more control over humans and the many resources of this planet and, frankly, this whole solar system."

"Well, do you think it could be a reason to kill someone?" Angie asked.

"People have definitely killed for much less," Brad replied. "So it's conceivable that someone wanted him out of the way or that he knew something someone didn't want to get out. But I'd rather not speculate at this point. We need time to dig a bit deeper."

As if to think about what he was going to say next, Brad was quiet for a moment before turning to Beth and saying, "I've decided to ask your mother to step in and accept the position."

Beth was stunned. "Why would you want my mom to take that job?" She felt a rush of sudden anxiety. The last person who had the position had just been murdered! And now he wanted her mother, her lifeline, to take the job?

"I trust your mother with my life. I've trusted her with your life. She's skilled in all ways necessary to do this job. If that element gets into the wrong hands, I don't know what could happen. But I do know it wouldn't be in the best interest of this planet or its many occupants."

Clearly seeing the panic written on his daughter's face, Brad took a step closer and spoke softly and directly into her mind. "We're far from our home, and our natural abilities aren't tied to this planet. In order to survive, we must be able to shift. We're bound by two souls, and both must be able to thrive. Or they'll tear each other apart. We'll disappear if the ink can't be made. This is about our survival."

Although they couldn't hear \ what was being said between Brad and Beth, the four guardians stood in what would become almost a sacred circle of beings. They could see the understanding of how serious this situation was slowly wash over Beth's face. This could truly be a matter of life or death for their kind.

After a few moments of silence, Michael cleared his throat to ask permission to speak. Brad, taking a step back from his daughter, turned his attention back to the group.

"Michael, I know you're going to need answers, and trust me, we'll get them. But right now I need the five of you to focus on the upcoming ceremony. The communing with our goddess hasn't happened for many, many years. Our fates are intertwined with that of humanity, and at this point we don't know where the danger may actually be coming from. So this ceremony is more important than ever."

Michael felt the weight of Brad's words press on his chest. This was all happening very fast. He was frustrated that there was so much about his existence that his father hadn't told him. But in a way, he supposed he was lucky. He couldn't imagine being Beth right now. Communion with the goddess was no small thing. Really, if he understood the tone of Brad's voice, it was everything.

"Is it possible for us to run the perimeter of the estate this evening?" Kia asked.

She was so small, Beth had almost forgotten she was there.

"Absolutely," Brad answered.

"Why don't the four of you meet me in the back courtyard, and we'll run it together," Dane said as he suddenly appeared.

"OK, how do you do that?" Beth asked while placing her hands on her hips like she was a child trying to figure out how a card trick worked. She was sure this time he hadn't used the garage door.

Dane simply flashed his brilliant cat-who-ate-the-canary smile while joining the group, making it clear he had no intention of answering her at this moment.

Beth, feeling very tired all of the sudden, turned to the group. "Yeah, why don't you guys go do that perimeter thingy, and I'll go lie down." Then she turned to her father. "Please tell me I don't have to shake everyone's hands goodbye," she said in an exasperated tone.

"Of course not. Go rest," he answered.

Feeling her eyes suddenly get very heavy, Beth feared she might not make it to her bed. Not only was her body overwhelmed with exhaustion, but so was her mind.

"You linked with four people today," she heard Kia speak in her mind. "You're drained and need to sleep."

"You're the guardian," Beth said with a smile. "So I'll take your word for that," she said out loud. *Linked?* she thought. That was a good word for it. That was exactly what it felt like—like she had an electric current running to each of them.

As they all filed out of the garage one by one, going their separate ways, Beth could feel that bond tighten. They might not be in the same room or even in the same house, but no matter where they were, Beth knew she would always feel them now. Her days of living as a solitary being were over.

SEVENTEEN

Beth recognized the white light that surrounded her. She could hear a faint hum off in the distance. She was asleep but no longer in her bed—or in her body for that matter.

"You're learning quickly," she heard Gabriel say.

"Which side are you on?" Beth asked.

She heard him chuckle. "Why are you so sure there are sides, Beth?"

"You said I learned quickly. So don't treat me like a child."

"But that's exactly what you are. A child learning to take her first steps, to speak her first words."

"Are you going to answer my question?" She knew that dancing around niceties and being polite was not the way to deal with him.

What is he? One of us? she wondered. Then she realized he wasn't a being of her world. *Is he some sort of angel?*

"Now you're getting closer," Gabriel answered, making it clear that if she thought something, he could hear it. "I can't hear everything. It will only be a matter of time before you learn to shield your thoughts."

"Well, thank god for that," Beth said out loud.

"God? Or goddess?" Gabriel was now walking in circles around her, literally.

Beth took note that it seemed to be more out of curiosity than to scare or intimidate her. Being careful not to break eye contact, she started to turn in circles as he walked. "As much as I love cryptic chitchat, don't you think maybe you could introduce yourself? And then maybe tell me where I am?"

Both were now stationary, standing shoulder to shoulder. Gabriel unfolded giant black wings that easily stretched the full length of a man. He continued to stare into Beth's eyes. As if his giant wings should explain everything, he lifted his eyebrows.

"OK, not really what I meant, but it's a place to start," she said.

"You don't seem frightened," Gabriel said with awe in his voice.

Beth now shuffled her feet, not sure where this awkward encounter was going. She replied, "With everything I've seen lately, adding an angel to the mix doesn't seem all that strange."

Chuckling, Gabriel grabbed a curly strand of her hair, then pulled on it and let it go, making it bounce. "Your hair was different last time we encountered one another."

Beth was starting to get slightly irritated with the fact that this seemed to be a one-sided conversation, and she took a step back. "OK. How about I ask a few questions, and you answer," she said.

"Shoot."

Beth laughed. She couldn't believe how nonchalant he was being. Maybe this was all in a normal day's work for him, but she was still having a hard time grasping that she'd been in her bed a few minutes before and now was standing in front of a giant winged man, reminiscing over hairstyles.

"Let's start with, What are you?" she asked.

"Oh, come on. You can do better than that. It's pretty obvious what I am."

"OK. You're an angel then?"

"Ding, ding, ding. Next question."

"Who exactly is it that you work for? *Was that right? Work for?* Beth thought. *How else would I say that?*

Gabriel laughed out loud. Clearly he was still eavesdropping on her thoughts. "Let's just say I answer directly to the gods and goddesses who are responsible for your extraordinary creation."

"Wait. There's more than one? Wow, this invisible world just gets bigger and bigger." Although she was talking more to herself out loud than to Gabriel, he still took the liberty of answering.

"I've heard you say that before."

"Right, OK. You've mentioned more than once that we know or knew each other. So can you please tell me how many lifetimes we're going on?

Clearly in a manner that suggested he was making fun of the question, Gabriel pretended to count on his fingers. "Well, this would be seven."

"Seven!" Beth practically shouted.

"Yes, seven."

"Why don't I remember any of these seven lives?"

"It's the way the game was designed," he said with a shrug.

"Game? What on earth?"

"Well, not always on Earth."

Beth had reached her limit with the mind-reading thing as well as with the cryptic answers. She could tell by the look in Gabriel's crystal-clear bright-brown eyes that he was amused by the little cat-and-mouse routine.

"OK, what game?" she asked. "This seems like it might actually be important, so please explain what you mean."

"Well, I can only say so much, per the rules of the game, but think of this as cosmic chess, and the Annu are most definitely the pawns." Gabriel leaned in as if to whisper in her ear with a sudden seriousness running through the tone of his voice. "Place your pieces carefully, and remember—each move may not always be what it seems."

And with that, Beth's eyes felt heavy as lead once again —too heavy to keep open. And with a sound that mimicked the rush of a fierce wind, she found herself shooting straight up out of her bed. Heart pounding and slightly disoriented, she realized she was safe in her room once again.

CHAPTER

EIGHTEEN

With her brain still reeling from her encounter with Gabriel, Beth sat on the edge of her bed, enjoying the early-morning sunlight that was coming through the window and warming her face. She was also staring at a large white box with a silver bow, which had been placed just inside her bedroom door more than a week before. But she hadn't yet opened it, as no one had mentioned its presence. Besides, she didn't have to look to know it was another new dress—probably for the ceremony that evening.

Ugh, the ceremony, she thought. Her stomach was in knots. This was all happening so fast. It had been two weeks already, and still no one had really discussed what would actually be happening at this ceremony. "Eating the apple" had been referred to more than once, but that was about it.

Deciding to finally take a look inside the box that seemed to be staring back at her, Beth placed it on her bed and removed the lid. "Holy crap!" she said out loud. Folded perfectly inside was a dress the most vibrant shade of red she'd ever seen. Its tiny sequins shimmered in the sunlight. Gently holding the straps, she lifted the dress from the box. It had spaghetti straps and an open back, and it looked as if it would hug her curves. As she held it up to herself, it flowed the length of her body, down to the floor. She was in awe of the material. She didn't know what it was, but it was the softest she'd ever touched. It reminded her of what a superstar would wear on the red carpet. Definitely designer.

It probably costs more than my mom's car, Beth thought.

She hung the beautiful gown up against the mirror on the back of her closet door. She was just about to head to the kitchen for some breakfast when she heard and felt the energy of some kind of explosion that created a large boom and rattled the glass in the window.

Dropping to the floor immediately with her heart pounding, fearful of another loud and intense bang, she crawled to the window and looked out just in time to see what looked like a giant shimmer flow from the back of the yard, and up and over the roof of the house, encasing the property in what looked like a glittery dome. She could also see giant eagles circling the house, letting out loud shrieks from time to time. They dove and dipped in what looked like a practiced formation.

Turning her attention back to the yard below, she took in a sharp breath. It was filled with the most beautiful wolves, mountain lions, panthers, and eagles. They were much larger than actual wild animals, and it was breathtaking to see so many in their animal form at once.

One wolf in particular caught her attention immediately. Without realizing it, she reached out with her mind and suddenly felt a wash of emotions come over her. No not emotions—these were instincts, much more powerful than just emotions. She could immediately feel the difference in Michael in his animal form. The link between them grew stronger by the second. She could feel his animalistic urge to run, to follow different scents, and the overwhelming need to protect.

As if to acknowledge her presence in his mind, Michael turned his head in her direction, making eye contact. His eyes were still his own but had a very wild quality that wasn't there when he was in his human form. Beth remembered what her father had told her. "We're bound by two souls. We must be able to shift, or they'll destroy each other."

A constant battle. One always trying to overwhelm the other, she thought as she stared into Michael's eyes. In that moment, she knew the wolf would most likely win that battle.

Pulling herself suddenly from the almost electric bond with Michael, Beth heard her bedroom door open. She jumped up off the floor, where she'd been hunching down and looking out the window, and saw Dane standing in her room.

"What was that earth-shattering noise?" she asked.

"Think of it as like a force field," he replied.

"A force field? Like on *Star Trek*?" she said with an almost childlike giggle.

Dane laughed. "Yeah, kind of like *Star Trek*. Humans wouldn't understand our ways and ceremonies. They'd be frightened. And when they're scared, they don't always think before they react. We must control what they see."

"So, we're inside a bubble that they can't see?"

"Well, they can see the house, but nothing else. From

the outside it just looks like a normal house with a normal yard at the end of a normal street."

Beth turned her attention back to the window, now seeing what looked like an oversized firepit being built. She also noticed that the large tent from the party the night before was gone, and torches were being placed every few feet to form a path headed in the direction of the firepit. All those who were in their animal form now sat in a large circle, with her four guardians in the middle.

"What's going on there?" she asked while pointing at the circle.

"They're getting their orders for security this evening."

"There's a need for security?"

"Well, we can't be too careful," Dane answered, taking a step closer to Beth so he could also see out the window. "It's important that everything go as planned this evening and that you're kept safe."

"What is it you think I'll find out this evening that's so important? And will someone please explain to me what will actually be happening at this ceremony? I mean, what is 'eating the apple'?'"

Beth realized her tone sounded a bit demanding, but really she didn't care. She was staring out the window at a bunch of people who had turned into giant wild animals and were being kept hidden under a force-field bubble. If she wasn't actually standing there seeing all of this with her own eyes, she never would have believed any of it. But that was also what made it all so amazing. The Annu, angels, guardians, and goddesses—it was a sort of comfort to know there was a bigger picture even if she didn't always see it. In a way, it made her feel less lonely to know there was a cosmic plan, or game as Gabriel had called it.

After taking a deep breath, Dane answered, "Tonight

you'll drink a special mix made by a great shaman of the Hopi people. There will be a prayer—well, actually more of a chant—that will begin as the moon enters and moves across the sky. You'll feel its power, you'll feel the resonance of the sound harmonize with the resonance of the Earth. When the moon reaches its highest point in the sky, a tear in the fabric of space and time will appear—a pathway to our goddess. A path only you can follow. What happens next only you will know."

"And when I come back through this tear?"

"I don't know. Like I said, only you will know what comes next. It's just my job to keep you safe before and after."

Pointing at the giant cat tattoo on Dane's arm, Beth asked, "Will I get my tattoo?"

"Yes, your spirit will reveal which animal you hold inside."

Beth thought back to her encounter with Gabriel. Seven times she'd lived and died. Seven times she'd played this game. Would all those memories come back tonight? And if they did, who would she be afterward?

Seeing the intense look on Beth's face, Dane turned her so they stood toe to toe and grabbed her shoulders. "I know it seems like the weight of a world you don't understand now sits on your shoulders. But remember this: regardless of what has ever been asked of you—no matter the task, no matter how large or how small—you've always excelled far beyond what's been expected of you. And this will be no different. You'll know what to do when the time comes. Trust in yourself, your people, and your goddess."

Beth smiled, grateful that with all the many changes over the past few weeks, some things remained the same.

She knew Dane would always be a steady figure in her life, just like her mother and now her guardians, as well.

Where's my mom? Beth wondered, realizing she'd hardly seen her the last two weeks and now not since the night before.

CHAPTER

NINETEEN

Kia sat in her animal form, listening as Brad and Michael gave everyone instructions regarding the security that evening. They would always be in pairs and take turns running the perimeter.

No one from the ceremony would be allowed outside the barrier for any reason once inside. The guardians would switch off. However, one guardian would always be with Beth from now until after the ceremony was complete.

Focusing on her link with Beth, Kia closed her eyes to follow the electric strand that ran between them.

Kia was looking forward to the ceremony that evening. After Beth received her tattoo, the bond among them all would be complete. Although they could speak to Beth with their minds, she couldn't answer unless she spoke out loud. The emotions ran only one way as well. She could feel them, but they could feel very little from her. Kia knew the importance of the bond being concrete. She didn't feel she could completely protect Beth without it. And that could be a reason for someone to not want the ceremony to happen. If the bond wasn't solidified, it might be possible to block the guardians from Beth's mind and make them unable to sense when she was in trouble.

"Kia? Kia! Any questions or things to add"?

Quickly pulling herself out of her thoughts, she realized Brad was speaking to her. Although he hadn't actually used his mouth to speak, his voice in her mind demanded an explanation through its tone.

"Something to add?" he asked again.

"I apologize, sir. I was simply thinking that it might be beneficial to some to stop the ceremony from happening. I mean, if our bond with Beth isn't completely concrete, it would be difficult for us to anticipate trouble."

This was the first time Kia or any of the guardians had seen Brad in his animal form, and it was more than a little intimidating. As a wolf, he stood at least a full head taller than the rest of the group. Kia didn't dare make eye contact; she simply bowed her head, keeping it low until Brad turned his attention back to the group.

"She's correct," he said. "That could definitely motivate someone to try and intervene this evening, and that can't happen. We all know what's at stake here. If Beth doesn't eat the apple this evening, the wolf moon won't appear in the right position again for seventy-five years, and that's not something we can afford. We know we have enemies. Though we may not know their faces, we know they're driven to succeed no matter the cost." As Brad finished, he looked directly at Michael, making it clear he was talking about the death of his father.

Michael let out a small whine and shifted his weight on his large wolf paws, acknowledging his loss publicly for the first time. At the same time, every wolf in the circle that surrounded the five let out a long howl that vibrated through the air and the ground, clearly expressing the pain they all felt at the death of one of their own.

As if on cue, at that very moment Michael heard the loud shriek of a bird. Looking up, he saw a group of eagles soaring high above them. They dipped, dove, and glided through the air, clearly doing what could only be explained as some kind of a drill. Memories of the eagle he'd seen move in the same way just before it dove to pierce his father with its sharp beak flooded his mind. Michael looked at each bird one by one. *Does any look familiar?* he asked himself. When they were standing directly in front of him, it was easy to tell them apart. Each person's soul shined through differently in the eyes, like fingerprints. No two were ever exactly the same. But Michael hadn't gotten that close to the eagle that murdered his father, so how would he ever find out who it was?

Turning his thoughts back to Brad's voice, Michael scolded himself, thinking, *Pay attention. Focus on the task at hand—keeping Beth safe. There will be plenty of time to find Dad's killer after Beth successfully completes the ritual this evening.* Realizing Brad must have been listening to his thoughts, Michael caught a quick nod Brad shot in his direction, as if agreeing with him.

"Consider yourselves all on duty from this moment forward. Keep my daughter safe. Do this not only for her but also for your people," he said in a very matter-of-fact voice. As he stood tall, with his hackles up, his posture reiterated that this wasn't a simple request. This was an order —the only order. "That's all. You're dismissed." Brad then left the group, still in his wolf form, and disappeared.

"Angie, you'll be on the front gate first," Eric said. "Kia and Michael, you'll run the perimeter and all the gates to make sure everything has been sufficiently secured with magic."

"When did you become the boss?" Angie replied in a playful voice.

Stumbling over his words a bit, Eric replied, "I— I— just figured because Michael is new ..." He tried to continue but was clearly too embarrassed.

"Calm down, silly. I was kidding. It's a good idea. Why are you so nervous? That's not like you," Angie said. It was then she realized why he'd been nervous. Quietly sitting and listening in her absolutely giant eagle form was Beth's mother. She was truly as beautiful as everyone had always said, but there was also something extremely dangerous in her giant talons and sharp beak. Kia noticed that she'd begun to tap her talon on the wooden perch she sat upon, a gesture that asserted her dominance and demanded respect. The four guardians immediately bowed their heads.

"I can appreciate the fact that some of you are just coming to terms with your new positions as my daughter's guardians," she said while looking directly at Michael and making it very clear she was speaking to him. Michael shifted on his paws and lowered his head. "But I'm here to tell you that absolutely no mistakes will be allowed this evening. Beth is my only daughter and the only one of us who can move this species forward. Her safety comes before everything—even your lives. So I expect you all to be focused and ready to defend her to just that point if necessary."

Kia nodded with the others, acknowledging everything Rena was saying while at the same time making a mental note that Rena clearly had a side she normally didn't show everyone. Her tone was sharp and protective, which Kia understood, with Rena being Beth's mother and all. But this felt like it was more than just fierce motherly love.

"If anything goes wrong, it will be her five guardians who are responsible," Rena said just before lifting her giant, majestic wings and taking flight. It was at that moment Michael noticed a small, beaded ornament fastened to one of Rena's talons. This in itself wasn't unusual; many of the Annu were decorated by beads, braids, and feathers, not only as people but in animal form as well. What seemed strange was that it was broken—a string of beads was clearly missing, leaving just the chain that once held them.

Thinking of it as nothing more than simply an oddity, Michael shifted back into his human form to continue helping others set up for the night's ceremony.

CHAPTER

TWENTY

Rena perched high above the house in a tree that reached higher than any other on the block. She watched in silence as her people ran from here to there, getting ready for her daughter's ascension to the goddess that evening. Rena knew there was no point in obsessing over what would actually happen during this ceremony. The ways of the goddess and her omens were always a mystery. She'd learned that young. Better to wait and watch before reacting.

Still observing from above, Rena saw Beth walk out into the courtyard. It had been only a few weeks since she'd met her father and been introduced to this strange world. Rena thought she looked older already. She walked with an air about her—the same air her father had as he walked. Rena had wondered if Beth would be angry with her for keeping such secrets all these years, but she was very pleasantly surprised that Beth seemed to harbor no ill feelings. She actually seemed to fully embrace her new world, no ques-tions asked. Rena chalked it up to intuition—Beth had

123

always known that she and her mother were different from others.

Since their arrival at Brad's house, Rena had been in the middle of some serious issues and hadn't been able to spend the time with her daughter that she probably needed to. She'd be at the upcoming ceremony, of course, because truly that was the only important thing at the moment. In all honesty, she was a bit overwhelmed. These serious issues weren't things that could wait, and they weren't things she could explain to Beth.

Feeling someone's intense stare, Rena looked down to see Brad in his giant wolf form, sitting quietly at the base of her tree. His eyes clearly conveyed that he wanted to have a word with her. Taking her time and staying in her eagle form, Rena jumped from branch to branch. As much as she didn't like Brad speaking to her through her mind and feeling her emotions, she wanted to remain in her animal form. Today, the eagle within her craved attention. The silence between them was anything but comfortable. The air was thick, and a type of tension hung between them.

"You've been gone," Brad said in a matter-of-fact way.

"And?" Rena replied.

"Our daughter walks with our goddess this evening, and you're nowhere to be found this morning." Again, not a question.

"Maybe you've forgotten that none of this works without that mine. The blue dust is what makes our survival here possible. Someone must step into the position of security with the death of the boy's father, and you made that person me." She wasn't in the mood to be treated as inferior, which was how Brad routinely treated her. This had always been a problem between them.

"I'm not asking to make you feel inferior. I'm asking

because our daughter needs her mother more than ever now. But most of all, I think you need her. In a sense, you're saying goodbye."

"Goodbye or not, she's ready," Rena replied with a sort of sigh. "She may have just found her guardians, but they have lifetimes of trust. They would each give their life for her. Especially Michael."

Brad chuckled. "We both know that relationship this time around will go much further than him just being her guardian."

"Maybe this time around we might actually get some grandchildren." Rena laughed, nudging Brad with her beak. "Someone will finally call you Grandpa."

"Hey now, let's not get ahead of ourselves. Do I look like a grandpa?" Brad replied playfully. However, the atmosphere didn't remain light for long.

"We've had a breach at the mine," Rena said. "A sample was taken."

"Which sample?"

"The only one that matters. The blue powder, fully processed."

Brad let out a low, guttural growl.

"I believe the boy's father found out who it was, and that's why they killed him," Rena said.

"They? You think this was the act of more than one?"

"Of course. They would need the cooperation of too many people in the mine to get it out."

"I have an idea where it was headed," Brad said. "A few months back, I was approached by the military—or at least people who were once military."

"What did they want?"

"What they always want. The powder and what that

blue powder possesses. They feel entitled because it landed on their planet."

"Well, maybe we should let them have it," Rena said with an exasperated tone.

"We can't. You know this. Look at what they've done with the technology they have—they murder by the millions, they let their own starve and die in the streets. Not to mention the planet itself."

"You yourself have acknowledged that this is their planet. Maybe we don't have the right to tell them no."

Shifting back into his human form and now speaking out loud and very directly, Brad turned to stare Rena directly in the eyes, as she'd also shifted back to her human form. He said, "They're not evolved enough to have something so powerful. There's a reason we don't let the half-bloods get their tattoos. They can't keep their emotions in check. They act without thinking, and at times thousands pay for it—even die for it."

Rena took a deep breath and opened her mouth to speak before closing it and simply saying, "You're correct, of course." Then she quickly shifted again and took flight high into the sky.

Brad headed back down to the fire being built. He had a very uneasy feeling in his gut. *Humans aren't ready for this power,* he thought. *Not to mention, we don't even know the full capabilities of the blue powder. This vial that's missing is a huge deal. And it's happening at the worst time possible.*

But Brad figured that was most likely by design. The vial had to be found, along with those who took it.

TWENTY-ONE

Rena circled high above the mine before landing directly at the security gate. There were three main levels of security to get into the mine. First, she'd had to shift and show her tattoo. Rena always thought it was a little ridiculous to have armed guards at the gate in human form. Gun or not, it would be difficult to stop a shifter in their animal form. They were fast, even faster than a human finger on the trigger. Not to mention they were large—much larger than they were in human form. How much damage would a bullet really do to a bear three times the size of any bear in the wild?

But still, even if a person made it through this first level of security, the second would be difficult to fake: an infrared scan of the eyes. Shifters had three times the pigment in their eye color, making their eyes more reliable than a fingerprint.

The third level was a scan under black light of the tattoo itself. It sounded easy enough to fake, but under the black light, the blue powder that was in the ink glowed. It didn't just light up—it actually showed the energy flowing through the tattoo and into the aura of the person, almost like smoke billowing from a fire.

Once Rena passed through the three checkpoints, she made her way down in the elevator to the bottom floor that was farthest underground—Level 7. The doors opened, and she rounded the corner, headed for the lab where all the blue powder was produced and stored. She was looking at the floor as she walked and suddenly bumped directly into Dane, smacking forehead to forehead.

"Ouch!" she growled before looking up and realizing it was Dane, who was rubbing his own forehead. "What are you doing here?" she asked in an almost hostile tone.

"Excuse me for bumping into you, but I'm here to collect your daughter's blue powder for her tattoo ink," he answered in somewhat of a shocked voice. It wasn't often he heard Rena speak that way, and never with him.

Taking a step back and looking rather exhausted, Rena said, "I'm sorry. It's been a long few weeks, and a lot rides on everything going smoothly with Beth tonight."

"All the more reason for you to be there with her now, helping her prepare."

Rena almost felt like she was being scolded, and she didn't like it. "I'll be headed back shortly, but I would appreciate it if you kept those 'fatherly' comments to yourself, as you're not her father."

Dane stepped forward and grabbed Rena, embracing her gently in a hug. She felt herself relax and took a deep breath in. Just for a moment, she pretended she was back at home, Beth was only ten years old, and it was just the three of them living a quiet life in Montana, where nothing much ever happened. She could almost smell the spring air when the grass was just sprouting after a cold winter.

Pulling herself back to reality, she let go of Dane, ran her fingers through her hair, and straightened her posture. "I'll see you back at the house in Chicago," she said.

Dane gave a smile and a wink, and just like that he was gone.

Rena sat for a moment, wondering why it was that certain males of their species could travel through thought and females couldn't—just like females could carry the soul of an eagle and a male couldn't. These were all questions she wished she could ask the goddess herself. In a way, she envied her daughter. She would speak with the creator. Would she be allowed to ask questions? Or was it simply a matter of listening to instructions?

Rena realized her mind had wandered and put herself back on task. She headed for a small door at the end of the hallway, knocking before hearing the many locks undo before the door opened. She entered a small lab that could probably hold only five to seven technicians at a time. She noticed that the male standing in front of her had the tattoo of a bear on his forearm. It was unusual to see a bear working in an intellectual position; their strength usually drew them to working in the diamond mines or security.

"What can we help you with, ma'am?" Rena heard a small female technician say. Both looked as though they were standing at attention.

"You can relax. I simply wish to see the logbooks from the past few nights—the book that shows where and with whom the finished product of blue powder goes."

"Yes, ma'am. The logbooks have all been gone through thoroughly. There's no discrepancy with the product leaving. It's just the count in the actual lab that's off by one vial."

Rena responded with, "And you've had no males who can travel by thought in the lab?"

"No, ma'am. But it wouldn't matter. The walls of the lab are made with copper. No one could travel in or out of the lab that way." Copper was the one element that could interfere with males' ability to travel by thought.

"I see. Thank you for your time." Then Rena left the lab and headed over to the visual security office. Again, as she entered the room, everyone stood immediately, like they were at attention.

"Keep working, everyone. I was just hoping to see the video logs for the last few nights."

"I can help you," a voice from the back of the room answered. With that, everyone went back to whatever task they'd been working on. Rena went to the back of the room to the female who'd answered.

"What's your name?" Rena asked.

"Hillary, ma'am."

"You may call me Rena, Hillary."

"Yes, ma'am. I mean Rena," the girl, with a wildcat tattoo on her arm, replied, making Rena chuckle. "Rena, if you're looking for footage in regard to the missing vial, I'm sorry to say you won't find it."

"How do you know this?"

"At Brad's instructions, I myself went through all the videos for the last two weeks, and, well, there's only one discrepancy."

"Which is?"

"Two nights ago we had a thirty-minute break in footage that was looping, so there's no way for us to see what should have actually been on that footage."

"Which cameras?"

The small girl, who looked to be as young as Rena's own daughter, suddenly looked very uncomfortable. Rena simply stood silently while waiting for an answer.

"Well, all of them."

Momentarily taken aback, it took Rena a minute to answer. "Thank you for your time, Hillary. You may return to work."

And with that, Rena left the room and then the mine altogether. The sun was getting low in the sky, and she needed to get back to Beth. But at least now she knew her secret was truly safe. No one was able to see her operative leave with the vial.

CHAPTER

TWENTY-TWO

Beth decided to take a walk out to the ceremony site before starting to get ready. She wanted to see it during the daylight hours before the sun set and the torches were lit. As soon as she exited the house, she could hear fire. Looking up, she saw a large pyre burning at the end of a stone path. It was so large, she thought it looked like it would burn forever. Suddenly, her father was next to her. Strange—again she hadn't heard him approach.

"Are you nervous?" he simply asked.

"Only a fool would say no to that."

He laughed and said, "You're ready. Of that I have no doubt."

"Well, that's reassuring to hear," Beth replied in some-what of a jovial tone. "I mean, what's really the worst that could happen? I get stuck with our goddess and get to spend my days playing games with the people of the world? Doesn't sound so bad to me."

Her father laughed again while turning to look up at Beth's bedroom window. "Your mother is here, and the sun is getting low. You'd better get ready. People will be arriving soon."

"People? How many people" Beth prayed it wouldn't be hundreds like the night she'd found her guardians.

"No, nothing like that," her father answered in her mind. That was one thing she couldn't wait to finally be able to do. It was irritating not being able to answer a voice in her mind.

Again her father laughed. Clearly he'd picked up on that twinge of irritation. "Go on. Your mother is waiting," he said.

Beth took one last look at the courtyard that would soon be the place where she left this world, and turned around to head back upstairs. As she walked through the house and headed back toward her room, her eyes suddenly felt very heavy—heavy like lead was weighing them down. Beth immediately knew she was about to travel to see Gabriel.

She managed to grab the wall next to her, but it felt like her arm went straight through it, and suddenly she heard that laugh. There was no mistaking it.

"Hello, Gabriel," she managed to say as her dizzy head slowly steadied itself and she saw she was standing on, well, nothing, But still, she was standing and could walk on this nothingness.

"Ahh, she speaks first this time."

"If you're trying to be cute—"

"Not cute. Factual." He circled her as if she were prey. "Actually, this whole visit today is simply to help prepare you with facts," Gabriel said while being very animated at the same time. He had an air of excitement around him that Beth couldn't account for.

"What kind of facts?" she asked dryly.

"Good question," he answered in a hurried manner while moving very close to her face. They were mere inches apart. "The kind I don't like, because it makes me look like I'm choosing sides."

"It seems to me you've already chosen, or I wouldn't be here."

"Ding, ding, ding. She's correct again!"

"Well then, let's get on with it. In case you've forgotten, I'm expected someplace this evening."

"Oh, no. I haven't forgotten," Gabriel said, suddenly becoming very still, quiet, and serious.

He walked behind her and stood for just a moment before leaning in to whisper just one word into her ear before she felt her eyes get heavy again. She knew she was leaving.

"Jump," he whispered. "Jump."

TWENTY-THREE

Beth pulled on the beautiful red gown that she'd been told had been made especially for that night. *It's truly a work of art*, she thought.

Looking in her bedroom mirror, she barely recognized herself: her dark hair was pulled partway up, with curly tendrils falling down her back. Earrings that almost looked iridescent but were surely real diamonds hung from her ears at just the right length. She had makeup on, which made her feel a bit strange because she never wore the stuff. Really, she didn't need it—her skin never broke out, her lashes were long (definitely longer than the average girl's), and her cheeks always had a glowing hue of pink. But tonight all those features were accentuated.

She was ready. Her heart pounded in her chest as she realized how close she was actually coming to going through with this. Not to mention her cryptic meeting with Gabriel. Beth shook her head and tried to clear her thoughts. *Focus*, she thought. *Focus on putting one foot in front of the other.*

At that very moment, there was a knock at the door.

"Oh, I thought my mother would be walking me down," Beth said as Dane opened the door.

He smiled as he stepped into the room. "She'll meet us downstairs. She had a few things to check on." In truth, Dane didn't know where Rena was, but the moon was getting higher in the sky, and Brad had said they couldn't wait for her when he instructed Dane to bring Beth down.

"OK. Well, I'm ready," Beth said, sounding very unsure of herself.

"Look at you. You absolutely are," Dane said with an almost fatherly tone in his voice.

Beth took a deep breath and followed him out of the room, down the stairs, and to the outskirts of the courtyard. Lit torches lined the way to the giant pyre that was burning just behind a small table, where a single cup and blade were sitting. Beth looked around. Not a single person was in human form except for what looked like a Native American shaman in full ceremonial dress standing by the small table. She could hear drums beating, although she wasn't sure where the sound was coming from.

"It's time," she heard her mother whisper. She was now somehow standing behind Beth, giving her a gentle nudge forward. Beth could feel all the eyes of every animal there staring her down as she began to walk forward. As she did, the shaman began chanting and dancing. It was mesmerizing, like he was calling for her, and she continued to walk.

One step after another, she got closer and closer to the shaman, and he got louder and louder. Pretty soon he was all Beth could hear or see. He didn't stop when she reached the table, and she could feel the heat burning high in the pyre just in front of her now. She felt like she was being pulled, but to where, she didn't know. Instinctively, she put her hand out.

Still chanting, the shaman picked up the knife and sliced her hand. Beth was so entranced with him and the heat that she didn't feel the blade. She felt the urge to pick up the cup that sat before her and drink. Slowly, and bleeding from her hand, she reached for it.

All of the sudden, as if shocked out of her trance by electricity, Beth heard several loud shrieks coming from the sky. Looking behind her, she saw chaos—animals running, fighting, and taking flight in every direction. It was as if she'd found herself in the middle of a great battle. The sound was deafening. She could hear and feel the panic in her guardians. She knew she couldn't help them, and before she even had a conscious thought, Beth let her instincts take over. She grabbed the cup and drank every drop from it.

At that very moment, she felt the ground beneath her start to shake. The colors swirled together as if to form a gray tornado that was moving in the wrong direction—not up, but down. Through the swirling storm, Beth could just barely make out bright blue. Then, what looked like bright-blue sky suddenly appeared in the ground in front of her. She could even smell salt from what she presumed was an ocean and hear, far away, what sounded like waves crashing.

Quickly pulling her attention from the blue sky and clouds right next to her feet, Beth looked up and saw a giant bear barreling toward her, yelling, "STOP HER!"

Then, she realized that animals in every direction were getting very close to her—angry animals that looked like they would stop at nothing to keep her from finishing the ceremony. She had no more than a split second to decide. She looked at the bear, looked at the vortex of blue sky, then heard only one word in her mind: *jump*.

So without a second thought and barely a moment to spare, Beth did just that. She jumped, even holding her breath as if she were jumping into a swimming pool. Looking up to where she'd just come from, Beth could briefly see the giant angry bear staring down at her as the vortex closed, leaving nothing but more beautiful blue sky. And all the while, she was still falling, and fast.

Beth couldn't help but think that this was brightest, bluest sky she'd ever seen. The color glowed like a freshly polished sapphire. But very quickly pulling her mind back to her predicament, Beth thought, *Oh man, wish I had some wings.*

And with that, she heard a musical laugh.

THE END of Book 1

ACKNOWLEDGMENTS

I would like to thank and dedicate this first book to a number of very special people in my life.

First and foremost, to my loving husband, Brian Caballero, who has always supported whatever crazy idea I got into my head and told me to go for it while standing beside me 100 percent of the time. I've learned so very much from you and feel so blessed to have you as my life partner.

Secondly, to my loving family—my mother, brother, and sister—who have always shown me nothing but support and unconditional love. I never would have started this journey without you.

To my beautiful children, Isa and Quinten Caballero. You inspire me daily and give me the strength to keep going.

To my father. Although you're no longer here, I feel your guidance and love daily. Thank you for all the life lessons.

Thank you to Jarmila Takac for the amazing cover artwork.

Finally, to my editor, Kristy Phillips. Thank you so much for all your hard word and guidance for a newbie. You went way out of your way to teach me what I needed to know, and I'm so grateful!